KB152850

L.I.E. 영문학총서 제 13 권

19세기 영미시인들의 소통에 대한 욕구

조 병 은

L. I. E. - SEOUL

2008

Preface

Whether it is a "spontaneous overflow of powerful feelings" or a painstakingly intentional creation, to a certain extent, all poetry aims at communication. To make effective communication possible, poets make many conscious efforts, from selection of materials and subjects, to employment of new techniques, and to versatile use of language.

Penetrating this collection of papers is the Nineteenth – Century poets' urge for communication. When poets feel a great sense of crisis in their lives and society as in the Nineteenth – Century England, they feel uncertainty in their role as poets and their search for a means of effective communication becomes desperate. And in the process, they want to confirm their place, literary and social, by seeking various ways. Many poets try to get away from the influence of their predecessors, to find their own voice and create their own poetic world. Since they want to find their individuality on which they can base their poetic vision, they want to find their own techniques to best express their inner desires. It is natural that, in the process, they become sensitive to the efficiency of language: they are often suspicious of the efficacy of language as a means of conveying truth, and try to find some alternative ways of communication, giving variety to language usage.

Sometimes, being sceptical of the referentiality of language, poets like Wordsworth break away from the 'poetic diction' of the previous age and resort to minimal use of language. Other times, they try to discover some new potentiality of language by mining the reservoir of collective consciousness or national history.

This book is composed of papers about these problems. In part one, papers show two poets, P. B. Shelley and Robert Browning, who make efforts to find their own voices by deviating from their predecessors' influence: they either 'mislead' their predecessors' texts or clearly declare their independence. Then, in part two, papers on two other poets, Matthew Arnold and Christina Rossetti, are presented who turn to the problem of self and try to find some basis upon which they may build their own poetic center, the core of their poetic vision. In line with the emergence of psychology in the nineteenth century, poets try to locate their poetic center in their buried self, create their own perspective to build their selves on, and forge a myth of their own. Part three is composed of papers on poems that deal with poets' sensitivity to the limitations of language. Since language is the primal means to communicate the poets' ideas and visions, they try to explore the function and effectuality of language. Realizing the limitations of language, some poets prefer silence to language, and others try to develop a new technique that, with minimal use of language, can have the maximum communicative effect. Robert Browning's dramatic monologue technique is representative of such conscious efforts to find a new way to render truth.

With the exception of a contemporary Irish poet, Seamus Heaney, all the poets in this book are Nineteenth century English poets. thus, the title *Nineteenth - Century Poers' Urge for Communication.* Through a reading of Heaney's "Glanmore Sonnets," I want to emphasize the fact that the urge for communication, as well as for redefining one's role in a rather complicated historical context, continues to be the primal concern in modern society, and more complicated in the case of Seamus Heaney.

Since the papers to follow were separately published in academic journals or university faculty journals, they are loosely related, though partly corrected and complemented; they might not have close – knit coherence and interconnectedness. But the very fact that we come to have access to the poetic concerns of those who were highly conscious of their roles and the functions of poetry in delivering truth provides ample justification for this collection.

I want to thank the Korean Society of Nineteenth Century Literature in English for offering me such a precious opportunity to publish this collection. Through this book, I hope to share my interest in the poets' urge for communication with many colleagues, both senior and junior, and students of English literature.

Finally, I want to express my thanks to my family for their never – ending invaluable support.

Early April, 2008
Byung – Eun Cho

Table of Contents

Humanities, Vol. 31. KangWon National University Press: Chuncheon, 1993) /107

2. Seamus Heaney's Exploration of Language in "Glanmore Sonnets" (*SungKongHoeDaeHak Nonchong: The Journal of SungKongHoe University. Vol. 8.* SungKongHoe University: Seoul, *1995.*) /126

3. "Anxiety of Communication in Browning's Dramatic Monologue, "Bishop Blougram's Apology"." (*"The Emergence & Development of Browning's Auditor."* Unpublished Dissertation. University of North Texas, 1991) /140

I. Over the Tradition

I − 1. "Overleap[ing] the Bounds" : The Quest for Ideal in "Alastor"

Perhaps more than any other of Shelley's poems, "Alastor" has been the center of critical controversies. Since Ramonds Havens declared in the 1930s that both the poem and its author "are confused," the main critical concern has been to find "some consistent way of unifying all the parts of the poem, the Preface, [and] the title into one coherent whole" (Cooper 63), with minor efforts to solve the "identity of the Alastor poet" and the meaning of love in the poem. Earl Wasserman comes to the fore among Shelleyan critics. If the New Critics, including Leavis and Eliot, blamed Shelley for the complexity and incongruity of the poetic voice and the poem, Wasserman accepts Shelley's split between scepticism and idealism, each represented by the Wordsworthian narrator and the Visionary Poet. He holds that the poem incorporates Shelley's scepticism by means of a dialectic between the two contrasting view points.

Starting from Wasserman, yet challenging him, recent deconstructive critics represented by Timothy Clark, Vincent Newey and Tillotma Rajan take the poem's resistance to closure, coherence and interpretation for granted and try to find a solution in the nature of the creative imagination, in Romantic irony, and in Shelley's "anxiety of influence." Clark, in his *Embodying Revolution* (1989), brings out crucial "relation between introspection and radical politics" from Shelley's representation of the poet – figure. For him, "Alastor," far from being a moral tale warning against the pursuit of solitude, dramatizes the destructive as well as creative potential of the revolutionary imagination. Newey emphasizes the dynamic nature of the work that reveals "Shelley's inner life, urges, confusions, and endeavor to work things out during a period of extraordinary crisis" (123).

He sees the opening portion of the poem as a "process of biblio – selving, a becoming in words, in which the young Shelley strives to establish a poetic identity that is distinctly his own and in fact does so by pointing out his difference from Wordsworth" (126). For Rajan, "Alastor" is not an ironic poem that incorporates two contrasting points of view: instead, it is "closer to being a work in which Shelley seeks to push back the encroachments of sad reality onto his beautiful idealism of moral excellence, and perhaps recognizing the impossibility of doing so, retreats into the moral censures of the preface without being able to abandon completely his view of the Poet as an ideal being" (255).

The purpose of this paper is to explore the process in which Shelley differentiates himself from Wordsworth and puts a cornerstone of a new poetic tradition on his idealism. Extending Newey's argument that, in"Alastor," Shelley shows his anti - Wordsworthian attitude, this paper attempts to show that his intentional "misreading" of Wordsworth is achieved by his presentation of the double perspective between the Narrator and the Poet. In the poem, Shelley follows what Bloom suggests as the fit process of achieving the strong poet's poetic ambition that "all strong poets develop their own identities by misreading their predecessors" (qtd. O'Neill 13). Shelley's strong "anxiety of influence" leads him to use no other poet than Wordsworth as his poetic mentor; then, his desire to establish his own creative identity urges him to "misread" his predecessor. Thus, in this poem, he deliberately employs Wordsworthian Narrator and borrows several passages directly from Wordsworth's poems to measure "aspects of his own situation and outlook" (Newey 124 – 5), and then, to repudiate Wordsworth in order to establish a new poetic tradition. For Shelley, Wordsworth and everything Wordsworthian is considered to be an object to overcome in order to stand on his own. Considering that this poem is one of his earliest poetic efforts, we can take such an approach as authentic and plausibly consistent with Shelley's idealistic tendency and the poetic situation in general.

"Alastor" is "the first effective treatment of the quest theme" (Hall 25), through which Shelley articulates his own notion of Romantic idealism.

Thus, an exploration of Shelley's idealism – what his idealism aims at, how he tries to achieve it, and what results he has – illuminates not only his poetic deviation from Wordsworth, but also his initiation into a new poetic tradition led by himself. In this respect, Shelley seems to be particularly ambitious and unusually determined. In "Alastor," Shelley's such distinctive idealism finds an effective "objective correlative" in the Poet's quest. In fact, to address the characteristics and quality of the quest theme, we should solve several specific problems that are closely connected with the Poet's search for the ideal: the identity of the veiled maiden, the significance of the Poet's search for the vision, and the evaluation of his isolation and his death.

The entire poem deals with a promising young poet, the Poet, an inspired solitary who is forever on the move, wandering around the world to seek for the vision that could fulfill the needs of his idealism. Distinctively derived from the basic notion of Romanticism – that "a person is essentially an idealist, and an idealist is a seeker, a wanderer, and a pilgrim who hopes to find something in the world worthy of (his/her) own high imaginings" (Hall 25) – the Poet's quest is, however, described in terms of ambivalence and confusion. That is, in the presentation of the way to pursue the Poet's idealism, Shelley takes an ambivalent attitude by building up a double frame of the poetic structure, and by taking a double point of view. Though it is a biological account of the Poet's life of quest, it is told by a Narrator whose view is not entirely sympathetic with either the Poet's or the author Shelley's. That the Poet's life is delineated by the Narrator can be a clue that he might be representative of Shelley's authentic voice. But Shelley's rather objective and critical comment on the Poet which is conveyed in the form of the "Preface" betrays such an expectation. Though accepting that Shelley is the overall controller of the entire poem, we cannot but feel a certain split in the perspectives and attitudes. On the whole, the author Shelley's attitude is ambivalent, inconsistent, and even confusing. On the other hand, he attempts, through the Poet's search for the ideal, to demonstrate his strong conviction that the ideal is worth pursuing, that it alone can illuminate a hopeful future on earth, and that in the light of the value of the ideal, even death does not matter. Instead of sacrifice, the Poet's death is recognized as a kind of self-realization. On the other hand, however, Shelley realizes that such a quest for the ideal, with an exclusion of communal value, has some implied danger of self-centeredness, which in most cases might bring a fatal result.

Such an ambivalence, in part, might be a reflection of Shelley's internal conflict between his desire and reality, his longing for idealism and his keen sense of reality and social responsibility, and even his desire for exile and his sensitivity to social demand for the poet which poets living in the Nineteenth century have commonly experienced. But at the same time, Shelley's ambivalent attitude itself is an effective strategical device through which he tries to camouflage his strong desire for originality and independence. By alluding to Wordsworth and borrowing passages from Wordsworth's poems, he tries to cover up his creative ambition. The entire poem, in this respect, records a process of Shelley's separating himself from Wordsworthian tradition. It can be understood as his "declaration of independence" from established mainstream poetic tradition represented by Wordsworth. Needless to say, in this poem, Shelley's self-defense is based on his emphatic stress of the value of a genuinely single-minded quest for the ideal.

Although Wasserman maintains that the two figures embody a split in Shelley's own aspiration – one poet for whom Nature, bound to finite world, is a beneficient and adequate context for humans, and another who rejects such Nature in favour of an impossible infinite perfection – at the beginning of the poem, they show a close kinship and affinity in their notion of nature.

The narrator – figure appears as a biographer and elegist of the idealized young poet. He both introduces the visionary Poet and inconsolably laments his death at the poem's close. He first appears invoking parental Nature for the inspiration that is to guide his elegy: "Mother of this unfathomable world!/Favour my solemn song, for I have loved⋯ " (11. 18 – 19). He feels motherly love and brotherhood with "earth, ocean, air" (l. 1). His conspicuously Wordsworthian notion of nature is shared with the Poet from whom "the magnificence and beauty of the external world sinks profoundly into the frame of his conceptions" (Preface). And their communion in nature continues until "the period arrives when these objects cease to suffice" (Preface). Then, the Poet's yearning for the mysterious journey starts, and Shelley's separation from the Wordsworthian notion of nature.

While Wordsworth sees nature in terms of its abiding interaction between self and an external organic reality, Shelley's relations with nature are altogether "darker and more risky than those of his predecessor" (Newey 126). In the first section of Shelley's address (ll. 1 – 17), where the phrase "natural piety" is adopted, nature seems to have "no actual presence at all, for the aesthetic and strongly erotic terms" – "dewy morn," "gorgeous ministers," "midnight's tingling silentness," "autumn's hollow sighs," "spring's voluptuous pantings" and "sweet kisses" – suggest the imagery of dream vision and longings of an isolate mind. Meanwhile, Shelley's nature is the projection of psychology and supernatural yearnings. His introduction of Wordsworthian phrases is only to repudiate his predecessor's notion of nature and emphasize his own idealism.

With relation to Shelley's idealistic position, "the central experience of the Poet and the determining event of the poem" (Hildebrand 16) is the vision of the veiled maid. Indeed, the veiled maid is the cause and, at the same time, the objective of the Poet's quest. Ever since the Poet has set his mind on the ideal, he has wandered all the old ruins and "undiscovered lands" to find it, until he sees a veiled maid in his sleep. Even since he has seen the vision of the veiled maid and achieved a passionate, though momentary union with it, he devotes his entire life to seeking it.

The vision of the veiled maid is a kind of "intuitive induction satisfying the acquired appetite for knowledge, truth, virtue, liberty and poesy" (DuBois 4). According to Gibson, the vision is an "epipsychidion" – "a soul out of his soul" (1026) emanated from the Poet himself, and not something outside his own nature. As the symbolic manifestation of the Poet's ideal, the vision of the veiled maiden has a function of synthesizing what the Poet has searched and is searching for: "the strange truths," "the thrilling secrets of the birth of time," and "knowledge, truth, virtue, divine liberty and poesy."

That the vision appears only when the Poet is prepared to meet it has significant implication to understand the condition and quality of the quest.

Prior to his experience of the vision, the Poet in the poem had spent his early youth in communion with nature, while traveling and studying philosophy:

By solemn vision, and bright silver dream,
His infancy was nurtured. Every sight

And sound from the vast earth and ambient air,
Sent to his heart its choicest impulses.
The fountains of divine philosophy
Fled not his thirsting lips, and all of great,
Or good, or lovely, which the sacred past
In truth or fable consecrates, he felt
and knew. (ll. 67–75)

Himself a Faustian figure, the Poet acquires a vast accumulation of knowledge and develops profound intellectual faculties. His readiness includes his ability to appreciate the "magnificence and beauty" of the world, and to modify his mind to "the infinite and unmeasured objects." For a certain period of time and as long as he maintains the Wordsworthian concept of nature and of humans' relationship with nature, he seems to feel satisfied.

But a yearning for "change" arrives to the Poet, the "change" that is simultaneously suggestive of Shelley's turn away from Wordsworth in his poetic goal and the process to fulfill the goal. In the poem, the Poet's discipleship of nature faces a turning point when he thirsts for "intercourse with an intelligence similar to himself" – "the Being whom he loves" (Preface). That he felt his fireside "cold" and his home "alienated" is a counter proof that such a familiar environment is not enough to fulfill his curious yearning for mysterious knowledge. Simply, he is now unable to be satisfied with "natural piety" that, as Wordsworth wishes in his poem, "Rainbow," binds one's days each to each to nature. And from this moment, his search for "strange truths in undiscovered lands" (l. 77) starts and, further, his split from everything Wordsworthian, from his notion of nature to his valuation of idealism for its own sake. The Poet's wandering through "many a wide waste and tangled wilderness" (l. 78), and "Nature's most secret steps" (l. 81), and "the awful ruins of the days of old" (l. 108) nourishes him to be mature. He wanders around and gazes on the old ruins of the world and pores over "memorials of the world's youth" till "meaning on his vacant mind/Flashed like strong inspiration, and he saw/The thrilling secrets of the birth of time" (ll. 126 – 8).

The rare and selective appearance of the dream vision as well as the identity of the veiled maid as a poet helps us define the nature of the Poet's quest. Shelley's description of the emergence of the vision of the veiled maiden is clear, gradual, and quite graphic. She appears in the Poet's sleep "in the vale of Cashmire." Sitting near him she "talks in low solemn tones" (l. 152). Not only is her voice like the voice of [the Poet's] own soul (l. 153), but also her theme, defined as "knowledge, truth, virtue, liberty and poesy" appears to him as the "thoughts that most dear" to him. Like him, she is "herself a poet" (l. 160), raising "wild numbers" (l. 163).

Clearly the prototype of the Poet, the veiled maid is identified with the "single image" evoked by the Poet himself through the union of "the intellectual faculties, the imagination, the functions of the sense" (Preface). As DuBois mentions, the vision of the veiled maid satisfies the Poet's "acquired appetite for knowledge, truth, virtue, liberty, and poesy" (4). All the "strange truths," "high thoughts," and even "the thrilling secrets of the birth of time" are included in the category of the maid's theme. They are converged into the embodied image of the veiled maid herself:

> Conservant with speculations of the sublimest and most perfect
> natures, the vision in which he embodies his own imaginations
> unites all the wonderful, or wise, or beautiful, which the poet,
> the philosopher, or the lover could depicture. (Preface)

If the vision of the veiled maid remained a pure vision, the Poet's search would assume an implausible naivety. That it was not so implies the realistic quality of his ideal. To the Poet, the vision assumes a reality going through a three-stage revelation. At first, she is recognized as a "concept" (Hildebrand 21), appealing to the Poet's "intellectual faculties" mentioned at the Preface. Hearing her talking, the Poet understands her elevated theme to be equivalent to his: "Knowledge and truth and virtue were her theme,/And lofty hopes of divine liberty,/Thoughts that most dear to him" (ll. 158 – 60). Then, as her mood changes and she kindles his imagination, she raises "wild numbers," creating "a strange symphony" on some "strange harp." He can also hear her voice "stifled in tremulous sobs," "the beating of her heart" and "her breath" that fills "the pauses of her music," all showing 'the influence of the imagination upon the affectionate phase of the soul (Gibson 1028). In the next stage, the veiled maid appeals to him sensually. When she ceases singing, the Poet turns and sees her "by the warm light of their own life" (l. 175). Beneath the "sinuous veil," he sees her glowing limbs, her bare "outspread arms," her "floating dark locks," "her beamy bending eyes" and her "parted lips" (ll. 176080), all, suggestive of "the perfection of sensuous details" (Gibson 1028). Thus, the vision is completed in perfect femininity, and she assumes an "ideal soulmate" (Gibson 1030), one who will respond to every quality of all three planes of "the intellectual faculties, the imagination, the functions of the sense" (Preface).

Shelley takes great pains to render the reality of the vision. He is meticulous in conveying its reality and thanks to his efforts, the originally shadowy figure, the veiled maid soon becomes the only reality, perhaps "more real than the Arab maid" (DuBois 540). For the Poet, once struck by the "unseen power" of the vision, the things that had occupied his attention fade into the light of common day and the vision becomes his only concern. It is no wonder that his ardent search for the ideal maid occupies the remainder of his life. Presenting a fatal experience to the Poet, the vision of the maid, both as the temptress and as the source of inspiration, becomes the only cause to which he dedicates his entire life.

That the veiled maid is conveyed as a poet figure provides a further clue to be connected to Shelley, the narrator, and the Poet, because all four of them were poets. The vision of the veiled maid is a mirror-like object upon which the Poet projects himself, and upon whom, in turn, is projected the narrator, and further Shelley himself. Such a layer upon layer of projected images of the poet is, to a certain extent, representative of Shelley's creative urge in which he tries to establish himself as a mainstream Romantic poet. In addition, all the poet-characters of the poem are respectively compared to the harp which makes sounds by the blast of the wind, the harp being a traditional symbol for Romantic poets. And by unifying the three persons into the single professional image of the poet, Shelley tries to combine the two inconsistent parts of the poem, the prosaic comment of the Poet's life in the Preface and the main narration of the poem.

Inseparable from the Poet's commitment to the ideal maid is his growing seclusion. It is not surprising that his dedication to the vision deepens his solitude, because one's pursuit of the ideal cannot go side by side with social activity. Thus, in his solitary wandering, he meets the vision of the veiled maiden; but, ironically, his meeting with the ideal "effected a greater solitude" (Hildebrand 32) in him. The Poet's solitude, hereafter, becomes an essential condition for the Poet's quest. As in many other romantic poems, such as in the Urizen of Blake, in the narrator of Wordsworth's "Excursion," in Coleridge's "Ancient Mariner," and in Keat's characters in "La Belle Dame," and "Fall of Hyperion," the Poet's "resort to vision cuts the visionary off from the human community" (Dawson 73). This seems inevitable because "the alternative to visionary escape could only be acquiescence in the conditions of the world as it was" (Dawson 73).

While accepting "solitude" as a prerequisite to a quest for the ideal, Shelley does not deny its negative impact, and in that lies Shelley's divergence from and criticism upon Wordsworthian solipsismal complacency shown in his real life. Recognizing that it is essential to achieve self – development and soul – seeking, Shelley seems to be extremely sensitive to the fact that the Poet's life of solitude conflicts with ordinary experience. Many critics, too, put much emphasis on Shelley's remark in the preface of the poem and identify the Poet's solitude with "self-love," a term obviously implying an egocentric attitude, the negative effect of which is clearly manifested in the Poet's premature death. Often going too far, critics have interpreted "Alastor" or "The Spirit of Solitude" as an evil power which drives the Poet to a "speedy ruin" by fostering his "self-centered seclusion."

Nevertheless, the Spirit of the Solitude, or "Alastor" repudiates any one –

sided interpretation. It has the same ambivalence as the Poet's quest because it is preconditioned by the nature of the Poet's idealism. Perhaps it is the dilemma of an idealist whose idealism starts from his/her disappointment with the present situation of reality, thus, whose desire is to change that reality through social reform or revolution in human consciousness. And this seems to be exactly Shelley's case. Clarke recognizes such dilemma of an idealist – poet and accepts the "necessary solitariness of the poet." For him, Shelley's remark in the Preface about the Poet's "self – centered seclusion" is understood as a sign of unease with which Shelley regarded the destructive imaginative processes that make their first appearance in "Alastor" (qtd. O'Neill 28). DuBois pays attention to the implied irony of the poem. Noticing that the poem is written from "the point of view of the earth – plane 'now'" (536), he maintains that, seen only in its earthly aspect, the Spirit of Solitude necessitates loneliness and death, by which it can be regarded as a malign power. But, he notices that the same spirit is identified with "the spirit of sweet human love" (l. 203) in the poem by its "virtuous function of rewarding the Poet with a vision of man, free, good, and beautiful" (536). Interpreting the spirit in such context, he concludes that the Spirit of the Solitude can be said to embody "the necessity of becoming and therefore the necessity of love" (DuBois 536).

A close examination of the Preface reveals that DuBois or Clark's stance is more consistent with what Shelley might have intended. In the latter part of the Preface, Shelley mentions "those meaner spirits" who are doomed to a "slow and poisonous decay":

> The Poet's self — centered seclusion was avenged by the furies
> of an irresistible passion pursuing him to speedy ruin. *But* that
> Power which strikes the luminaries of the world with sudden
> darkness and extinction, by awakening them to too exquisite a
> perception of its influences, *dooms to a slow and poisonous*
> *decay* those meaner spirits that dare to abjure its dominion
> (emphases added, Preface).

As Hildebrand rightly points out, the conjunction "but" is all important.
It "qualifies what Shelley really means about the Poet's solitude and his
early death" (Hildebrand 28). Although the Poet confronts a "speedy ruin,"
he is still a "luminary" by virtue of his vision, being awakened to "too
exquisite a perception of its influences." He only commits a "generous error"
which, from the immortal point of view, is not to be blamed, though not
commendable. "But" those who have no vision meet a "more abject and
inglorious destiny" for their "delinquency is more contemptible and
pernicious." Though they live longer, their lives are "unfruitful" ones.

Whether for creative reasons or for realistic reasons, the Poet's solitude is
presented as an inevitable burden to bear: "He lived, he died, he sung, in
solitude" (l. 60). Although the fatality of the Poet's solitude is reinforced by
the swan's flight home to his mate, it urges the Poet to fix his mind on a
search for the veiled maid. The more he recognizes his fatality, the more
desperately he sticks to the one-remaining choice, that is, the search for the
ideal vision. When he looks at a beautiful flower on his way, he is tempted
to enjoy its beauty, but "on his heart its solitude returned,/And he forbore"
(ll. 414-15). Until the end of his life, he remained by himself, as he remains

loyal to his single – minded quest. He assumes an ascetic stance toward pleasure in worldly affairs and nature.

The identity of the veiled maid illustrates that the Poet's quest for the ideal is either internal or beyond the bounds of the living world – whether it be death or a movement to a certain metaphysical realm. If the veiled maid represents something within the Poet, his search for her must be an internal journey. The long and highly ambiguous descriptions of the Poet's journey implies it. The Poet himself is aware of it, too. Going through the loss of vision – it is "lost, lost, forever lost,/In the wide pathless desert of dim sleep" (ll. 209 – 10) – he wonders whether the "dark gate of death" conducts him to the "mysterious paradise/[of] sleep" (ll. 211-12). Skeptical of his quest, he shows a mixed response to the possibility of failure in his quest: "The insatiate hope which it awakened stung/His brain even like despair" (ll. 221 -22). His mixed use of "hope" and "despair" without semantic distinction can be interpreted as a far allusion to the relationship between "life" and "death." For an idealist, death might even be the very means of life. Noticeably, the Poet's premonition of death is briefly expressed by the narrator: "He eagerly pursues/Beyond the realm of dream that fleeting shade. He overleaps the bounds" (Preface). Ironically, the narrator's unemotional tone embedded in the short sentence seems to reveal his fear, not to mention the Poet himself's, of the Poet's impending death.

The Poet's journey is intended to be "a kind of an emblem of provision of life" (Stevens). It becomes clear by the dominant water imagery, which signifies the Poet's quest towards the "mystical origins of life" (Stevens), specified by the symbol of a spring. Furthermore, in the scene where the

Poet reaches the cave, we learn that his death will be absorbed in an ideal realm in which nature's "cradle" is identified with the Poet's "sepulchre": "He sought in Nature's dearest haunt, some bank,/*Her cradle, and his sepulchre*" (emphases added, ll. 429-30). It is at this point that the Poet's death is understood in the wider context of a new birth.

With relation to the Poet's quest theme, one of the most important arguments revolves around the meaning of the Poet's death. In the poem, the Poet's death brings a culminating effect and the proper measure of the quality of his search. It is a "force within the poem every bit as powerful as love" (Cooper 64), and critical responses are varied. Some interpret the Poet's death in terms of life's fading and destruction; others see it as a positive element in its significance in the Poet's quest. Havens asserts that the Poet, right after the appearance of the veiled maid, only looks for suicide; Gibson holds that, after seeking vainly for a prototype for the vision, the Poet seeks for a place to die when he embarks on the shallop; DuBois says that the death is a cosmic necessity and the Poet, by accepting his death, triumphs over the fear of death (517); Hildebrand maintains that the Poet's death is not tragic to himself, but is to those who remain behind (61); Cooper remarks that "death is both the object of his search and the process (73).

These varied responses themselves show the extent to which the interpretation of the meaning of death totally depends on one's perspective. Instead of contemplating death as a physical fact, which would naturally be a terrible thing to a person as young as the Poet, we have to consider his death in the larger context of his quest – what significance it has to the quest. Indeed, the argument on the Poet's death qualifies not only the quality and validity of the Poet's quest, but also Shelley's attitude towards, and his relationship to the Poet.

The Poet's death scene shows us that his death is not a destruction to him. It is an opening to his becoming a part of nature. Not only is he initiated into nature as a new member, but he also changes the landscape of nature. By his visit for death, "the wild haunts" of the wind become the "depository of all the grace and beauty" (l. 594); the "murky shades" embrace his "silent, cold, motionless" dead body as "their own voiceless and the vacant air" (ll. 660-662); and the "dawn/Robes [his body] in its golden beams" (ll. 686-688). He joins to nature, by becoming a part of it. He is, through his death, canonized in nature on account of his utmost quest for the ideal.

Although the Poet's early death brings his quest to an end, it is not a thing to despair, but rather a thing to value. For the death is described as a transcendental state: "Hope and despair,/The torturers, slept; no mortal pain or fear/Marred his repose" (ll. 639-41). It is no wonder that he meets his death peacefully: "he lay breathing there/At peace, and faintly smiling" (ll. 644 – 45). The Poet's death is not a natural death, but a "natural process" (Hildebrand 42), a means to achieving freedom. It is not a waste or termination of everything: it is rather an ultimate consummation of life in search of the ideal. On this account, our estimation of the Poet's death should be based on our evaluation of the quality of his life, that is characterized by a consistent search for the ideal. What is important is not the fact that an individual meets an early death, but what we come to know about his life which was composed of a single – minded search for the ideal.

Death is meaningful not because it tells the Poet's departure from the earth, but because it testifies the quality of his life.

The narrator's lament on the Poet's death may easily lead us to a rash conclusion that Shelley commits an error of sentimentalism by allowing too much space and effort in pouring out his sorrow. But when we consider that through one's death can we shed light on one's life as a whole, the narrator's mourning for the Poet's death should be interpreted as Shelley's effort to render significance to the Poet's life and to value the quality of his search.

Shelley's position is clear from the Preface and is backed up by the entire atmosphere of the poem. Shelley believes that there are two ways to die — either gloriously, like the Poet who remains loyal to his vision, or miserably, like those who abjure the vision. To emphasize such belief, he adopts two similes to distinguish the two. After the Poet's death, the narrator says that people "[either] go to their graves like flowers or creeping worms" (l. 602). He also mentions that "many worms and beasts and men live on" (ll. 691-92) after the Poet's death, yet, the Poet is safe "from the worm's outrage" (l. 702). From this context, it is obvious that Shelley intends to suggest that the Poet dies "like flowers" which are expected to be born again in the next spring, whereas "those meaner spirits" die "like worms" and perish to feed the flowers.

The narrator's overall attitude toward the Poet further confirms such an attitude. After the Poet's death, the narrator calls him "the brave, the gentle, the beautiful,/The child of grace and genius" (ll. 689-690) and one of the "surpassing Spirit,/Whose light adorned the world around it" (ll.

714-15). For the narrator, the Poet, during his life, was a "luminary" by virtue of his vision, and of his consistent search for the ideal, whose death is considered as shocking as to "turn their lights to shade" (l. 715). The Poet was also a "missionary genius" whom Shelley so much esteemed to be a proper model of the poet who functions as an 'unacknowledged legislator of the world.'

The evaluation of the Poet's quest in Shelley's "Alastor" rests on the fact that he remains loyal to his ideal. He consumes himself in search of the vision that might bring "truth, beauty, virtue, liberty and poesy" on earth. Although his search ends with his physical death, his premature death preconditions his immortality by joining him to nature. By his death, the Poet assumes a role in the grand status of nature by becoming a part of it. Perhaps the fact that such a "surpassing Spirit" has once existed on earth may give some hope for the future of human beings. The Poet's quest for the ideal is, in this sense, to be recognized as an affirmation of the value of an ideal pursuit and a kind of self-realization on the Poet's part.

In the same context, for Shelley, the best way to separate himself from the Wordsworthian influence is to emphasize his idealism, and Shelley succeeds in it through his in-depth exploration of the quest theme and through an interplay of the two texts of the main poem and the Preface to the poem, of the poem and the prose, and of the Narrator and the Poet. His skillful manipulation of the Wordsworthian view of nature through the Narrator and his direct quotation from Wordsworth's poems serve his purpose magnificently. By contrasting two perspectives of the Narrator and the Poet, Shelley successfully differentiates his view of nature from that of

Wordsworth and by focusing on the Poet's single-minded quest for the ideal, he prepares an independent way to stand on his own.

To sum up, the double perspective of the poem is not a manifestation of Shelley's confusion or split between scepticism and idealism. It emphasizes the extent to which Shelley's craftsmanship serves his poetic ambition. His presentation of the double perspective is thus to be understood as an effective device to "misread" Wordsworth in order to find a new poetic voice, and further to create a new poetic tradition initiated by himself, while residing in it as a base. And that is what Shelley ultimately achieves by his creation of an extremely Romantic poem that idealizes a search that "overleaps the bounds."

< Works Cited >

Brisman, Leslie. *Romantic Origins.* Ithaca & London: Cornell Univ. Press, 1978.

Clark, Timothy. "Destructive Creativity: Alastor (1815)," *Shelley*, Ed. by Michael O'Neill. London & New York: Longman, 1993.

Cooper, Bryan. "Shelley's 'Alastor': The Quest for a Vision," *Keats-Shelley Journal*, 19 (1970), pp. 63 – 76.s

Dawson, P. M. S. "Poetry in an Age of Revolution," *British Romanticism*, Ed. by Stuart Curran, Cambridge Univ. Press, 1993.

DuBois, Arthus E, "A Note on Intuitive Experiences," *A Study of Alastor*, Ed. by Hildebrand. Kent: Kent State Univ. 1954.

DuBois, Arthus E. "Alastor: The Spirit of Solitude," Journal of English and *Germanic Philology*, 35 (1936). pp. 530 – 45.

Gibson, Evan K. "Alastor: A Reinterpretation," *Publications of Modern Language Associations*, 62 (1947). pp. 1022 – 45.

Hall, Jean. The Transforming Image: A Study of Shelley's Major Poetry. Chicago: Univ. of Illinois Press, 1980.

Havens, Raymond D. "Shelley's *Alastor*," *Publications of Modern Language Associations*, 45 (1930). pp. 1098 – 1115.

Hildebrand, William. *A Study of Alastor*. Kent: Kent State Univ; 1954.

Keach, William. "Obstinate Questionings: The Immortality Ode and *Alastor*," *Wordsworth Circle*, 12 (winter, 1981). pp. 36 – 44.

Newey, Vincent. *Centering the Self: Subjectivity, Society and Reading From Thomas Gray to Thomas Hardy*: Scholar Press, 1995.

O'Neill, Michael, Ed. *Shelley*. London & New York: Longman, 1993.

Rajan, Tillotma. "Idealism and Skepticism in Shelley's Poetry," *Shelley*. Ed. by M. O'Neill. London & New York: Longman, 1993.

Reiman, Donald & S. Power, Ed. *Shelley's Poetry and Prose*.. New York & London: W. W. Norton & Co; 1977.

Steinman, Lisa. "Shelley's Skepticism: Allegory in 'Alastor'," *English Language History*, 45 (1978). pp. 255 – 269.

Stevens, Robert. Unpublished Lecture Notes on "Shelley and Other Romantic Poets." Denton, TX: Univ. of North Texas, 1988.

Wasserman, Earl. *Shelley: A Critical Reading;* Johns Hopkins Univ. 1971.

I − 2. In Search of Poetic Independence: A Reading of Browning's "Pauline"

Critical response upon Browning's first published poem "Pauline" has been quite controversial. The main controversy revolves around the genre of the poem. On this issue, Browning scholarship has divided into two distinctive camps. On the one hand, scholars considered "Pauline" as a pure lyric and subjective poem, which is, in DeVane's expression, "thoroughly autobiographical" to the extent that "Browning is the speaker, hardly disguised at all" (*Browning Handbook* 42). On the other hand, represented by Roma A. King Jr. and Park Honan, Patricia Ball, and Michael Hancher, more recent criticism has tended to veer in the opposite direction and maintains that the poem is objective and dramatic, representing "the interior life of a character, not that of the poet[Browning] himself" (Roma King 3).

In one way or another, neither position seems to do justice to the poem, often leading the readers to several misconceptions. For one thing, the first group of scholars tend to depend too much on J. S. Mill's review of the poem. They take Mill's apparent identification of Browning with the poetic speaker in terms of an extremely "self-conscious poet" so much for granted that they not only slighted "Pauline" from their discussions of Browning's poems, but also tended to draw a strict line between the poem and Browning's later poems. They concluded that Mill's marginal comment on the poem marked a turning point in the direction of Browning's poetry so that Browning has drastically changed the direction from a subjective and self – indulgent Romantic tendency to an objective, and dramatic technique.

The second group of scholars committed similar mistakes. Although they presuppose that "Pauline" is a dramatic poem, their position is primarily based on Browning's own remarks. They literally take Browning's defensive remark which was added to his 1864 edition of poetry: "The thing was my earliest attempt at poetry 'always dramatic in principle, and so many utterances of so many imaginary persons, not mine'" (qtd. Erickson 25).

Correcting some of the misunderstandings that would be caused by any biased view of the poem, this paper attempts to show that the focus of the poem lies in more about Browning's search for a dialectical poetic mode that would incorporate both personal and impersonal elements than about his exclusive subjectivism or about his complete transformation of it, and that is to be read as a declaration of poetic independence on Browning's part. His rather extreme admiration of Shelley is, in this context, also to be read as a preparation for his gradual getting away from the latter's influence toward a more independent creative activity.

Browning's such effort is in close line with the predominant social situation of the Victorian period. Without doubt, on the threshold of a new poetic era, Browning had to solve the Victorians' artistic dilemma between two conflicting claims, the Romantic legacy of expressive subjectivism and the new demand for objectivity and social enlightenment in poetry. Major Victorian poets confronted the same dilemma and each had to find a way through which he/she could come to terms with the two equally demanding claims. Tennyson sought a solution in his acceptance of the poet laureateship, reconciling his inclination to aestheticism with his public role as the national bard. Disappointed by the inadequacy of poetry in coping with social requirement, or more accurately, by the lack of poetic sensibility of the Victorian readers, Arnold had to shift his profession from a poet to a social commentator and a prose writer.

Browning's effort to accommodate such a social demand without completely sacrificing his subjective element is epitomized in his search for a dialectical mode of poetry with the posthumously attached terms, "dramatic monologue." It appears from his first published poem "Pauline" (1833) and reaches its apex in his mature dramatic monologues. Generally, it takes a two-way track: on the one hand, he objectifies the poetic speaker, gradually eliminating the poet's subjective elements in the poem; on the other hand, he incorporates the auditor figure into the poetic context in an effort to objectify and authenticate the speaker's poetic utterance and to procure the readers participation in the poetic process.

Especially noticeable in "Pauline" is Browning's conscious effort to associate the issue of overcoming Romantic legacy with the auditor figures. Browning employs more than one auditor figures in the poetic context and make quite a versatile use of them for conveying his changing attitude towards the Romantic legacy: he expresses and, at the same time, transforms his inherent Romantic tendency in terms of the shift of the auditor figures in the poem.

The first auditor, Pauline, helps create dramatic situation of the poem. Weaving an outer frame of the poem, she complements the otherwise quite subjective articulation of the poetic speaker, himself a poet just like Browning. Conveying Browning's notion of what kind of a poet he would like to be in the future, Pauline becomes an "intermediary between the speaker and the reader" (Thomas 28). In short, she provides some degree of objectivity to the poet's otherwise direct self-revelation to the reader. Taking various roles, she helps the speaker's understanding of himself and his poetic mission.

Af first, Pauline appears as a modified muse who, instead of being an abstract and divine entity, plays the role of the speaker's lover. The opening passage is characterized by its emotional intensity and pictorial vividness. Though following the epic invocation of the muse, this passage stresses and, more accurately, defines the auditor, Pauline, in terms of a physicality that verges on Keatsian sensuality:

> Pauline, mine own, bend o'er me — thy soft breast
> Shall pant to mine — bend o'er me — thy sweet eyes
> And loosened hair and breathing lips, and arms
> Drawing me to thee — these build up a screen
> To shut me in with thee, and from all fear;
> So that I might unlock the sleepless mood
> Of fancies from my soul, their lurking — place,
> Nor doubt that each would pass, ne'er to return
> To one so watched, so loved, and so secured. (ll. 1-9)

Pauline's irresistible physical presence with her "soft breast," "sweet eyes," "loosened hair," "breathing lips," and encircling "arms" brings in several points that make the poem crucial in Browning's career. Certainly, the emotional immediacy and emphatic corporeality of the auditor not only become the very source of the dramatic quality of the poem but they also provide a standard to measure Browning's divergence from, even more than his overall indebtedness to, Shelley.

To several scholars, the auditor Pauline's physicality offers a clue for the originality and inventiveness of Browning's dramatic technique. Comparing "Pauline" to its alleged matrix, Shelley's poem, "Alastor," Park Honan has linked Pauline to the "veiled maid" by her multiple roles as "a lover, as a source of protection, and as an alter ego" (Honan 15) to the poet-hero. Meanwhile, in his unpublished dissertation entitled "The Premise of Browning's Dramatic Monologues" (1979), Carl Bandelin has also identified Pauline with figural characteristics of the Shelleyan maid. Nevertheless, as Honan has properly emphasized, "Browning's significant innovation was the introduction of a *living audience* for his hero's story in the shape of Pauline" (emphases added 15). As the poetic auditor, Pauline occasions the speaker's confessional narrative in which the latter can "lay his soul bare in its fall" (l. 124) and "strip [his] mind bare" (l. 260). Furthermore, as a living audience, Pauline can act out what the speaker wants her to do for him. Her role exceeds that of the "veiled maid." Pauline does not remain an image but emerges to be an agent figure by and through whom the speaker can attain spiritual awakening based on confidence, consolation, and a sense of security she provides. She is the one who is able to bring in changes to the disillusioned speaker who is "ruined" (l. 89) and trapped in himself, "in shame" (l. 28), and in what he has pursued in his youth, that is, in "wild dreams of beauty and of good" (l. 30).

The dramatic immediacy and pictorial vividness of the opening scene, however, soon yields to involuted sentences and a complex poetic structure which accompany the speaker's rather tedious outpouring of his personal history. Instead of taking Pauline as his conversational counterpart, in the ensuing narrative, the speaker is absorbed in a one – sided confession of his pride, sin, and moral confusion. As a result, the vitality of Pauline's role as the immediate poetic auditor is suspended and she exists as an emanation of the speaker's "buried life" (Shaw 10) or a "prolongation of the [speaker's spiritual] dilemma into the present" (Honan 16) than as a distinctive auditor figure who is capable of responding.

Rather than being an immediate object of the speaker's persuasion, Pauline undertakes a role which is more closely linked to the speaker's creative activity, in particular, his creation of this very poem, entitled "Pauline." And by joining Pauline into his creative process, Browning endows this poem with metapoeic function. By charging Pauline with a crucial role in the composition of this poem, Browning places her at the "organizing center" (Honan 15): he "dedicate[s]" the poem to her, beginning and ending it "through [her" (l. 871). As the "necessary person for whom the imagination is exercised" (Walsh 11), Pauline occasions the speaker's "Fragment of a confession," guiding, directing, and more often challenging his perception of self, poetry, and faith. Weaving the poetic irony through her comments in French which are added to the speaker's self-indulgent effusion after line 811, Pauline plays a vital role in shaping a double context of the poem as a commentator or an "editor" (*Becoming Browning* 26) of the poem.

More significantly, by putting his narrative center in Pauline, Browning achieves other poetic objective: he sketches his future poetic orientation through Pauline. This is explicit in the speaker's plea to Pauline in which he wants her to be what Shelley had been to him and is now to the world: " – so/Wast thou to me, and art thou to the world!" (ll. 189-190); which is also indirectly expressed:

> And my choice fell
> Not so much on a system as a man –
> On one, whom praise of mine shall not offend,
> Who was as calm as beauty, being such
> Unto mankind as thou to me, Pauline, – (ll. 403-409).

Throughout the poem, the speaker elevates Pauline's imagined role, while partially discrediting his previous hero, Shelley. From the speaker's point of view, the entire poem is thus an enactment in which he changes his position from Shelley's "listener" (ll. 410-413) to a speaker with Pauline as his listener, and in which Pauline's position changes from the speaker's unrewarded lover to his lately-acclaimed protector and listener. In other words, the poem presents a process of the speaker's defamiliarization of revision of his past life, which has been overshadowed by Shelley, in favor or reconstructing the self back from the alternative source, i. e. through Pauline.

Such a transition is marked by the speaker's panegyric appeal to Shelley, by calling him in extremely idealized terms, the "Sun-treader" (l. 151). By this invocation, his disclaimer of Shelley takes a form of valediction and personal ritual. The basic reasoning is simple: since "[Shelley is] gone from us" (l. 152), "never to return" (l. 159), the speaker inevitably has to turn to his long – forgotten lover, Pauline. Still not quite believing that Shelley ultimately left him (l. 161-71), the speaker attempts to find his consolation in Pauline whom he deserted in his youthful pursuit of the Shelleyan ideal – [his] hopes of perfecting mankind,···faith in them···in freedoms's self/And virtue's self, then my own motives, ends/And aims and loves, and human love" (ll. 458-461). With Pauline as his listener and by "look[ing] again to see if all went well" (l. 468), he wants to "set [the] final seal/To [his] wandering thought" (ll. 107-108), while "supply[ing] the chasm/'Twixt what [he is] and all [he] fain would be" (ll. 676-677).

That Shelley, in contrast to Pauline's physicality, appears as a spirit, pure and unreal, a non-historical or legendary figure further supports Browning's ambivalence toward Shelley, as well as illustrating his poetic strategy concerning his search for independence. That is, Shelley's spirituality, his physical absence, fits the poetic scheme in the same exquisite way that Pauline's physicality works as an apt demonstration of Browning's innovative treatment of the auditor figure. With relation to the speaker's transition, it has more to do with Browning's ambivalent attitude toward Shelley than with Shelley's premature death. On the one hand, by presenting Shelley as a spirit, the speaker implies his deliberate, though reluctant, distancing of himself from Shelley, both emotionally and poetically. On the other hand, the speaker expresses his unwillingness to accept Shelley's physicality at all, perhaps even in his lifetime, because he was for him such an ideal itself whom he worshipped rather unconditionally when young.

The speaker's extreme idealization of Shelley as a symbol of immortality may, in part, be a reflection of his reluctance to accept human mortality, which itself provides an important motive for any artistic creativity. His occupation with mortality further becomes overt when he wishes for Shelley's immortality in such wishful passages as "life and death be thine for ever!" (ll. 208-209), and "live thou forever" (l. 1027). For the same reason, the "fear" from which the speaker wants Pauline to protect him might imply his fear of death – death as has become reality by his departure from Shelley, the embodiment of immortality. Even the speaker's final wish that Shelley "be near him" (l. 1024) "chiefly when [he] die[s]" (l. 1025) can be interpreted as expressing the same repulsion from death and his consequent reluctance to part from Shelley as the source of immortality.

Juxtaposed, the two auditor figures, Pauline and Shelley, embody polarities of the speaker-poet's attitudes towards faith, love, and poetry. As the poetic auditor shifts from Shelley to Pauline, the poetic movement proceeds from what Shelley signifies to all that Pauline means. Shelley has been Browning's spiritual mentor with his professed atheism, his pursuit of love for love's sake, his single-minded quest for redemption through self, his subjective approach to poetry, and his dream of universal emancipation from all kinds of tyranny. On the contrary, with her unique status as the speaker's lover, Pauline represents practical domestic love, faith in God, a more objective treatment of poetic subject – which is represented by Pauline's notion of a perfect bard as one who "chronicled the stages of all life" (l. 883) – and above all, his "soul's friend (l. 560)," "breath, life, a last/resource, and extreme want" (ll. 907-908) and a "help" (l. 930). In the speaker's transitional process leading to his final declaration of belief in

"God and truth/And love" (ll. 1020-1021), Pauline turns out to be a necessary instrumental figure whose role is so much emphasized that she became a Pauline," a general term allusive to Paul in the Bible who brings changes to others' lives.

Interpreting the poem as a record of Browning's practice of what Bloom called "anxiety of influence," Bandelin has elevated Pauline's functional significance as the speaker's poetic audience. According to him, Pauline fulfills a double auditor role for the speaker, replacing two kinds of listener:

> She replaces the Suntreader as an intimate companion, creating a scene of discourse in the natural world that corresponds to the imaginary scene of which Browning stood with Shelley in some more sublime imaginary realm. She also replaces the larger public audience that Shelley has pre-empted. (81)

In spite of his perception and critical insight, Bandelin misses seeing the speaker's lingering indeterminacy represented in his alternate return to both Shelley and Pauline. He has not taken into account Browning's ambivalent attitude towards either Pauline or Shelley, nor has he considered Browning's inner motivation of such hesitance. Consequently, he disregards the emotional subtlety and internal conflict involved in the speaker's transition from Shelleyan Romanticism to contemporary poetic demands.

A valid ground for the speaker's necessity for a vacillation in his departure from Shelley may still be explained in terms of "anxiety of influence," but with its cause and effect reversed. According to Bloom, the original notion of the "anxiety of influence" is the posterior poet's "deepest desire··· to be an influence than to be influenced" (12) by the precedents. This notion presupposes the later poet's initial revolt against the inherited poetic convention or influence in order to become an influence himself. Of course, the final result might be the same 'independence,' but Browning's motivation seems to be predominantly emotional rather than rational, more based on a sense of loss than on a philosophical or poetic speculation, and thus more arbitrarily self – directed than supported by logic.

David Latane's explication of Browning's motive for his departure from Shelley is further illustrative of the speaker's emotional situation. In an article entitled "Shelley's 'Baneful Influence'" (1983), Latane defines Shelley's influence as "baneful" and contends that

> Browning's turning away from Shelley may be an instinct to jump off a crowded bandwagon, one associated publicly with an embarrassing cult, and privately with a youthful though anonymous folly, rather than a complete or systematic repudiation of Shelley's art. (33)

In conjunction with such emotional, rather than logical separation, the poem illuminates two things. On the one hand, the speaker's departure based on his private motive helps elevate Pauline's status to a more solid and functionally credible than she might otherwise have had. For, it is no other than Pauline who is emotionally involved with the speaker, that is, by love. On the other hand, the speaker's emotion – based determination conditions his position to be vulnerable and tenuous, which causes, and partially excuses, his lack of commitment. Lurking behind his oscillation between the two auditor figures lies his emotional unrest and psychological indetermination. Likewise, despite his self-imposed spontaneity, the speaker's departure is situationally forced by Shelley's world-wide recognition and by Browning's reluctance to share in public his personal idol with others.

The first stage of the speaker-poet's swerve from his poetic and spiritual mentor, Shelley, assumes his revisionist approach to the latter's imagery. This becomes clear in his use of the image of a fountain. Browning borrows this image from Shelley's poem "Mont Blanc" and modifies it to suit his theme when he explains the speaker's belated learning of Shelley's public fame and influence. In "Pauline," the spring, instead of being the original tenor for mysterious poetic origins or poet's mind, or for the symbol of the Platonic Idea, becomes the poet's secret and private source of inspiration which he cherishes

> As one should worship long a sacred spring
> ......
> And then should find it but the fountain – head,
> Long – lost, of some great river washing towns
> and towers···. (ll. 172-180)

The poet's adherence to the image of seclusion as a private space with his personal idol continues when he wants Pauline to replace Shelley, providing him with a similar retreat he once had with Shelley. Just as the sacred spring indicates his private source of inspiration, the "silver thread" that has broken away from its parent – river and finally joins it functions as a channel to the speaker:

This is the very heart of the woods all round
Mountain – like heaped above us; yet even here
One pond of water gleams; far the river
Sweeps like a sea, barred out from land; but one –
One thin clear sheet has overleaped and wound
Into this silent depth, which gained, it lies
Still, as but led by sufferance;
···.so, at length, a silver thread
It winds, all noiselessly through the deep wood
Till thro' a cleft-way, thro' the moss and stone,
It joins its parent-river with a shout. (ll. 766-780)

In more direct, but equally figurative passage, the poet-speaker is compared to a star – watcher who is now "altered," "worn," "weak," and "full of tears" by Shelley's being "world renown." Reminding one of the modern day 'star – fan relationship,' the context renders the intensity of the shock and the irremediable sense of isolation, loss, and betrayal that the speaker undergoes because of Shelley's publicity:

And now when all thy proud renown is out,
I am a watcher whose eyes have grown dim
With looking for some star which breaks on him
Altered and *worn* and *weak* and *full of tears*.
(emphases added, ll. 226-229)

The main signifier, "watcher" is crucial in linking the speaker to Pauline who is also described as one "so watched, so loved, so secured" in the opening passage of the poem. By using the same signifier for the two different subjects, Browning puts the speaker in the same position as Pauline as a passive victim.

Meanwhile, Browning carefully and gradually builds a close kinship between Shelley and Pauline, particularly in terms of their respective relationship to the speaker. In an extended simile of a girl, Browning presents Pauline as a sort of Freudian counterpart to Shelley. In the first two quoted lines, he substitutes the speaker's sense of guilt for an irreducible sense of loss and unabated nostalgia:

> And, I, perchance, half feel a strange regret
> That I am not what I have been to thee:
> Like a girl one has silently loved long
> In her first loneliness in some retreat,
> When, late emerged, all gaze and glow to view
> Her fresh eyes and soft hair and lips which bloom
> Like a mountain berry; doubtless it is sweet
> To see her thus adored, but there have been
> Moments when all the world was in our praise,
> Sweeter than any pride of after hours. (emphases added, ll. 191-200)

The remainder of the quotation is concentrated on Browning's meticulous construction of the affinity between Shelley and Pauline in the speaker's life. The girl in the poem who has "silently loved long/In her first loneliness in some retreat" appears to be an unmistakable reminder of Pauline. When she came out from the secret retreat, this girl was transformed into worldly "adored," going through the same process that Shelley had experienced before he became "renowned." Inferring from Browning's parallel of Shelley and Pauline by simile is the speaker's synchronic fusion of the previous and future objects of commitment into one. As Bandelin argues, this figural assimilation of Pauline and Shelley might be an "attempt to impose coherence on the psychological turmoil" (76) of the speaker-poet. By juxtaposing the two figures, Browning creates an illusion of seamlessness in the speaker's life, a sense of continuation that facilitates his psychological transmission and adjustment from one to another.

At a more positive level, the speaker's effort to compensate the loss of a private idol, the "Suntreader," is documented in his search for a unique poetic style. Browning transforms the speaker's reluctant but unavoidable compromise of his personal idolatry with poetic hero worship into a fit opportunity for confirming his independence and equal standing with other poets. Then, he could not only stand on his own, but could become renowned like Shelley himself. After all, a new discovery of his compatibility and ability to create his own visionary world might mean a better compensation and exaltation of self than anything else:

> ⋯.so I sought to know
> What other minds achieved. No fear outbroke
> As on the works of mighty bards I gazed,
> In the first joy at finding *my own* thoughts
> Recorded, *my own* fancies justified,
> And their aspirings but *my very own.*
> With them I first explored passion and mind.
> − All to begin afresh! I rather sought
> To rival what I wondered at than form
> Creations of *my own;*; if much was light

Lent by the others, *much was yet my own..* (emphases added,
ll. 383-393)

With recurrent uses of the first person possessive pronoun, "my own,"
Browning transforms the speaker's departure from Shelley into a new
initiation into original and independent art.

Then, as the speaker confesses to Pauline, he accepts his changing attitude
toward other poets as toward himself as a poet:

····witness my belief
In poets, though sad change has come there too;
No more I leave myself to follow them –
Unconsciously I measure me by them – (ll. 691-694)

It is, however, only after "having made life [his] own" (l. 700) that the
speaker is sure to be "prepared" for being an objective poet who can "tell
[his] state as though' twere none of [his]" (ll. 585-586). With Pauline as a
vehicle for a change, the speaker – poet finally acquires self-confidence as a
professional poet. Likewise, he now can stand with other poets, having
clearer poetic vision and without having any fear or shame:

····I shall live
With poets, calmer, purer still each time,
And beauteous shapes will come for me to seize,
And unknown secrets will be trusted me
Which were denied the waverer once;
I shall be priest and prophet as of old. (ll. 1014-1019).

In the speaker's compensation of emotional loss with his poetic gain, Pauline and Shelley respectively become the emblem of the opposing notions of "the verse being as the mood it paints" (l. 259) and of the verse "chronicl[ing] the stages of all life" (l. 884), of Romantic and Victorian notion of poetry, and of the abstract and the practicable reality.

Ten years after the poem "Pauline" was published, Browning outlines a poet's development in three stages in his "Essay on Chatterton" (1843):

> Genius almost invariably begins to develop itself by imitation.. It has, in the short-sightedness of infancy, faith in the world; and its object is to compete with, or prove superior to, the world's already recognized idols, at their own performances and by their own methods. This done, there grows up a faith in itself; and, no longer taking the performance or method of another for granted, it supercedes these by processes of its own. It creates, and imitates no longer. Seeing cause for faith in something external and better, and having attained to a moral end and aim, it never discovers in itself the only remaining antagonist worthy of its ambition, and in the subduing of what at first had seemed its most enviable powers, arrives at the more or less complete fulfillment of its earthly mission.. (emphases added, qtd. Erickson 24).

The three – stage development of 'imitation – creation – achievement of earthly mission' can be taken as summing up the process the speaker – poet of "Pauline" has undergone. In the poem, he "sought to rival" (l. 391) before he formed "creations of [his] own" (l. 392), and then, he confirmed his poetic mission as a "priest and prophet of the world."

At the end of the poem, the speaker's return to "Sun – treader" is quite important because it indicates his confidence in his relationship with Shelley. It marks a manifestation of his final position as an independent poet:

> Sun-treader, I believe in God and truth
> And love; and as one just escaped from death
> Would bind himself in bands of friends to feel
> He lives indeed, so, I would lean on thee! (ll. 1020-1023).

By this passage, the speaker not only asserts his belief in "God and truth/And love" (ll. 1020-1021), but also shows his self-confidence and readiness to take Shelley as if he is a "friend" to him.

Browning's achievement in his first poem "Pauline" lies in his search for a proper auditor type that would fit his poetic purpose. He employs more than one auditor figures to convey his poetic orientation, which mainly consists of his departure from Romantic legacy of subjective approach to the poetic materials. He employs and mobilizes each auditor figure in a way that would be expressive of a certain aspects of his dilemma as a poet and serve his poetic aims. Especially, his creation of the living auditor in the shape of Pauline deserves special attention, because she prefigures the auditors in Browning's more maturer dramatic monologues. Though limited in her function and delineated in amorphous profile, she objectifies the poetic situation and connects the poem with Browning's more maturer poems. And in that respect, she plays a sort of unifying element of the poem. King's comment on Browning's employment of Pauline seems to summarize such a position: "The creation of Pauline, in spite of her insubstantiality, is a genuine triumph" (9).

Thematically, "Pauline" occupies a significant position in Browning's career that exceeds the poem's initial importance as his first published work. In it, Browning rehearses his departure from and transformation of the Romantic legacy, which is expressed in more definitive terms in another of his poems, "Sordello" (1840). In terms of the poetic mode, "Pauline" marks a transition of Browning's interest from a strict traditional dichotomy between lyric and drama to a dialectical mode, the dramatic monologue. However incomplete, the status of "Pauline" as Browning's seminal effort for his envisioning of the dramatic monologue is crucial.

< Works Cited >

Ball, Patricia M. *The Central Self: A Study in Romantic and Victorian Imagination.* The Athlone Press, Univ. of London, 1968.

Bandelin, C. F. "Browning and the Principles of the Dramatic Monologue," An Published Dissertation. Yale Univ; 1979.

Bloom, Harold. *A Map of Misreading.* New York: Oxford Univ. Press, 1975.

Browning, Robert. *Poetical Works 1833 - 1864.* Ed. by Ian Jack. London: Oxford Univ. Press, 1970.

Collins, Thomas. "Shelley and God in Browning's "Pauline": Unresolved Problem," *Victorian Poetry* 3 (1965): 151 - 160.

Crowell, Norton B. *A Reader's Guide to Robert Browning.* Albuquerque: Univ. of New Mexico Press, 1972.

DeVane, W. Clyde. *A Browning Handbook.* New York: Appleton - Century - Crofts, 1955.

Erickson, Lee. *Robert Browning: His Poetry and His Audiences.* London: Cornell Univ. Press, 1984.

Hancher, Michael. "The Dramatic Situation in Browning's "Pauline"," *The Yearbook of English Studies* 1 (1971): 149 - 59.

Honan, Park. *Browning's Characters: A Study in Poetic Technique.* New London: Yale Univ. Press, 1969.

Jack, Ian. *Browning's Major Poetry..* Oxford: Clarendon Press, 1973.

Keenan, Richard. "Browning and Shelley," *Browning Institute Studies* 1 (1973), 119 - 46.

King, Roma A. Jr. *The Focusing Artifice:: The Poetry of Robert Browning.* Athens, Ohio: Ohio Univ. Press, 1968.

Latane, David. "Shelley's 'Baneful Influence', " *Studies in Browning and His Circle* 11 (1983): 31 - 36.

Pekham, Morse. "Browning and Romanticism," *Writers and Their Background*: *Robert Browning*. Ed. Isobel Armstrong. Athens, Ohio: Ohio Univ. Press, 1975.

Ryals, Clyde de. *Becoming Browning: The Poems and Plays of Robert Browning 1833 - 1846*. Columbus, Ohio: Ohio State Univ; 1983.

_____*The Life of Robert Browning*. Columbus: Ohio State Univ; 1993.

Thomas, Donald. *Robert Browning: A Life Within Life*. New York: The Viking Press, 1982.

Walsh, Thomas P. "Browning's "Pauline": The Fiend in the Cave," *Studies in Browning and His Circle, 21* (1997): 9 - 22.

Woolford, John & D. Karlin. *Robert Browning*. London & New York: Longman Group Ltd, 1996.

II. Creating the Self

II - 1. "The Buried Self" : The Central Self in Matthew Arnold' s Creative
Imagination

Search for the self has been one of the oldest themes of literature.
Regardless of whether one lives in a rather established society with
pretty-well fixed systems of thought, or in a fluctuating society with often
catastrophically dynamic changes, one feels, at least at a certain period of
life, the necessity to search for the self: one wants to confirm who one is and
what one's goal of life should be. Such a yearning becomes especially urgent
at a period when one experiences a sense of crisis in life, either personally or
socially, which, in turn, incites one to a confirmation of the self.

As far as the self as a literary topic is concerned, in no period were people
more enthusiastic and more repudiating than in the Victorian period. If, in
the Romantic period, search for the self was an open and legitimate literary
activity and the notion of the self was elevated and exalted, considered to be

privileged and all – important, the Victorian interest in the self has been shown to be complicated, ambiguous, and often paradoxical. It is represented in the gap between people's enthusiasm for the self and the way to articulate it, between an eager search for, and an intentional avoidance of, the self. This means that, in literary activity, one has to distinguish the direction of thinking from the mode of expression, and the content from the form of literature. If the flourishing development of the Bildungsroman and the exploration of the mental substrata in psychology are marks of Victorians, enthusiasm for the self, a series of new techniques and strategies in writing reflect their conscious refusal of subjectivity in favor of an objective treatment of literary ideas.

Writers tried to find means, either literally or socially, to come to terms with such a dilemma in their creative environment. To take the three main poets of England, Tennyson found a social solution by fulfilling his role as the Poet Laureate, a public shade under which he could continue his subjective lyricism; Browning experimented with various materials and techniques in search of an objective mode, eventually inventing the dramatic monologue technique; Arnold, taking a public position as a school inspector, sought for a mode of writing fit for the demand of the period, which finally resulted in prose criticism, and tried to locate the kernel of his ideas in the notions of culture and humanism.

The basic assumption of this paper is that Arnold's search for the "buried self" or "buried life" occupies a central part of his effort to find a literary solution to the problems of the period such as the dissolution of religious faith, the permeating sense of loss, general depravity, alienation, etc. In several poems including the one with the same title, "The Buried Life," the concept of the "buried self" functions as a controlling metaphor from which a series of Arnoldian tenets and attitudes towards life such as "self-dependence," "resignation," and "disinterestedness" evolve.

Upon such a premise, this paper is intended to trace the process by which Arnold puts the notion of "the buried life" at the center of his literary activities, considering it as a bridge point that connects his poetry to prose writings and endowing coherence for his works. Compared to its importance in the development of Arnold's ideas, the notion of "the buried life" has not received proper critical attention. It was either disregarded completely or, at most, was picked up and soon discarded. In order to carry out an extensive argument, this paper will focus on "The Buried Life," a poem which has been equally ignored and underestimated, but which deserves to be evaluated as a thesis-poem in Arnold's literary activities, a thesis poem in the same way as a thesis-sentence in writing.

Occupying the central position in the "constellations of poems from which Arnold's idea of the self emerges" (Stange 168), this poem spreads out various phases of the "buried self" through his other poems and prose writings. In this poem, Arnold incorporates his idea of the "buried life" in terms of its meaning and implication, its functional efficacy, and its unaccessibly evasive quality. Even though Arnold's effort to define the notion of the buried life appears unsystematic and somewhat sentimental in this poem, none can deny its thematic importance in Arnoldian canon. In the same context, though rudimentary, with random appearance, and "not [quite] elevated" (Stange 172), the "buried self" acquires a solid position, putting a cornerstone in the more sophisticated concepts such as humanism and culture.

In fact, fidelity to the "buried self" appears so important in Arnold's poems that, in proportion to [one's] "desire either to know or to avoid knowledge of the hidden self" (Stange 173), the characters either choose a life of self-dependence and resignation, or they simply renounce the existence of the "buried self" and preoccupy themselves with their social roles. Consequently, Arnoldian poetic land is occupied with only two types of people, "madman" and "slave": a "madman" is the one who revolts against the "world" in Byronic defiance, and a "slave" is the one who subdues himself to the world and leads a life of "quiet desperation." Both being extreme types, they are defeated alike, "one by the finite in the world, the other by the infinite in himself" (Culler xii) and prove that "the madman is as much a slave to his own passion as the other is to the world" (Culler xii).

Particularly noticeable in such a dichotomy is that, to a certain extent, every person is tempted by a double inclination to a knowledge of the "buried self" and a deliberate or habitual renouncement of this self. For Arnold, this vacillation is not only derived from the specific situation of the Victorian society, but it also constitutes the existential condition of humanity. In order to avoid circular repetitions of such vacillation and not to let the human beings fall into an existential labyrinth, Arnold prescribes the "buried self" as a source of authority in his notion of the self, in his creative activity, and in the emerging problems of the period. His primary task is to establish the notion of the "buried life" as a tenable position by retrieving and objectifying its existence. Then, he would take hold of it as a sustaining prop. Arnold's yearning for objectification of the "buried self" contains a difficulty of definition and communication, the poet's consciousness of which, again, offers itself as a momentum for poetic creation.

For Arnold, the act of defining an already-existing notion is as significant as that of creating a new one because, by definition, he can endow a vague notion with substantial reality and transform it into something substantial – something, in the Victorian context, that would either be an alternative to or replace, in its function, the Christian faith, the sway of which was greatly weakening at that time. Inseparable from that, Arnold seems to have a clear notion that an abstract mental entity such as the "buried self" cannot and should not be carried in the unsatisfactory vessel of language. After all, language is too limited to contain human minds.

Such a double consciousness – the necessity of and, at the same time, the impossibility of complete verbal definition – governs, like two poles, the poetic atmosphere of "The Buried Life." In the first section, it becomes more complicated, being combined with the flippancy of the love relation between the speaker "I" and his lover. The implied tension is between expectation and reality, between what love should be and what it is, and between read[ing] thy inmost soul and "our war of mocking words":

> Light flows our war of mocking words, and yet,
> Behold, with tears mine eyes are wet!
> I feel a nameless sadness o'er me roll!
> Yes, yes, we know that we can smile!
> But there's a something in this breast,

To which thy light words bring no rest,
And thy gay smiles no anodyne.
Give me thy hand, and hush awhile,
And turn those limpid eyes on mine,
And let me read there! thy inmost soul. (ll. 1-10).

Here the combined infertility of love and meaninglessness of articulation loosen the human bond between lovers. In this context, this part of the poem assumes an elegy, lamenting the loss of conventional romantic love that idealizes perfect unity and a 100% communicability between lovers; thus, a "nameless sadness o'er me roll." In a romantic and at once anti – romantic situation, Arnold's immediate concern is to what extent one's inmost soul can be communicated in words. His presentation of the communication block between lovers – in which the beloved's words "bring no rest" and her smiles give "no anodyne" to the speaker – is quite intentional: On the one hand, he questions the efficiency of language in conveying the reality of human thought; on the other hand, from such a communication block, Arnold reads the possibility of the "buried self." "the common stream" beyond the shifting appearance. Instead of the communication degenerating into "wars," the speaker implores his lover to "hush a while···And let [him] read there ··· thy inmost soul."

Set against the "war of mocking words" and the "inmost soul[s]" repudiation of verbal definition, a generic notion, a supposedly common conception is suggested, giving vent to the poet's yearning for true communication. It is something inherent in, and essential for human existence, but at the same time, evasive, indivisible, and hard to be within one's grasp. It even exists prior to linguistic sifting or selective reasoning process. It lies buried deep in a realm into which words cannot penetrate. For the poet, who is quick to realize "love as a means of alienation" (Honan 228), this generic notion would throw light on how to "unlock the heart" and "reveal/To one another what indeed they feel." This same heart that "beats on every human breast" would replace the harsh reality of human relationships which is replete with "blank indifference," blaming of others, various forms of disguises and one's loneliness among men as well as to oneself, being "alien to the rest/Of men, and alien to themselves":

> Alas! is even love too weak
> To unlock the heart, and let it speak?
> Are even lovers powerless to reveal
> To one another what indeed they feel?
> I knew the mass of men conceal'd
> Their thoughts, for fear that if reveal'd
> They would by other men be met
> With blank indifference, or with blame reproved;
> I knew they lived and moved
> Trick'd in disguises, alien to the rest
> Of men, and alien to themselves   and yet
> *The same heart beats in every human breast!*
>
> (emphases added, ll. 11-23).

Throughout the poem, Arnold applys various terms either directly signifying or indirectly implying "the buried life" and its function, ranging from the vaguest notion of "a something" (l. 6) to the "inmost soul" (l. 11), "the heart" (l. 13), and "the same heart" (l. 23), and to the "genuine self" (l. 36), and "our hidden self" (l. 65), and "the buried life" (l. 48). In addition, he uses several layers of metaphors, all related to the metaphor of water, and each moving toward the definition of the "buried self," from "the unregarded river of our life" (l. 39) and "the buried stream" (l. 42), to "our true, original course" (l. 50) and "our own line" (l. 60), and to a "lost pulse of feeling" (l. 85), and "the life's flow" (l. 88).

Employing various terms representing multiphase of the "buried life" Arnold gradually illuminates the entity of the "buried self," while, by his consistent use of the metaphor of water, compensates for the lack of centrality of the former. As Buckley maintains, the metaphor of water, implying some "permanent values above and beyond the shifting conflict" (102), may indicate Arnold's yearning for conversion, some dramatic solution, quite familiar to Victorians, that would put an end to his sense of crisis and of the meaninglessness of life.

From Arnold's amorphous use of terminology, one can conjecture that Arnold himself might have suffered from the same negative experience of love which he could not quite overcome at the time when he wrote this poem. He might have felt the same sense of loss in his love affair (presumably with Marguerite) and the same urge for something to turn to. In any case, the notion of "the buried self" or the "buried life" presupposes Arnold's keen consciousness of the disparity between past and present in both his personal life and the society he lives in. His sense of the present instability accompanies an opposing sense that "things were not always this way" (Miller 215). Rapid changes in several areas such as industrialism, democracy, science, capitalism, and urbanization have contributed to rendering the age "arid," "barren," "blank" and "unpoetical" and to deprive one of true selfhood.

The general sense of loss permeating in the Victorian society has to do, in part, with the loss of the Romantic notion of the self. Sypher maintains that the privileged Romantic self, in its last stage of development, had to deal with the problem of the communal role of the self demanded by the Utilitarian concept of "the greatest good for the greatest number" and had to yield its predominancy, resulting in a loss of the very self that maintained the Romantic ego. For the Victorians, not only did annihilation of the Romantic self leave a void in their view of life and the world, and deprive them of their position in the universe, but also, to make matters worse, in such an embarrassing moment, they had to encounter still another self that led their everyday lives, an existential self emerging from the ashes of the Romantic self. To meet its existence and to cure the people's puzzling vacuity, writers had to propose something, for Arnold, something that is inherent, inaccessible, and buried deep and that is to be evolved as "the buried self" (Sypher 19-33).

Personally, Arnold himself experienced a deep sense of loss after his graduation from the university. According to his biographer Park Honan, Arnold suffered from a crisis of identity which was caused by "lack of faith [which made] him unsure of himself and his purposes" (147). Honan's illustrations include Arnold's sensitive response to an increasing imbalance of mental faculties between thought and feeling, to his disappointment in his sister Jane's insipid response to his poems – his sister, mentioned "K" in several of his poems, and the "only witness"······to the possibility of "that abiding inner life" (103) – and his deep sense of loss caused by his father's sudden death and his brother Tom's emigration to New Zealand – Tom, who had "behave[d] as Matthew's alter-ego" (Honan 121). In addition, Arnold's reading of Oriental writings including Hindu scriptures, as well as his access to Emerson's notion of "Over-Soul," stimulated his interest in and search for the "buried self." Honan suggests that, by establishing the concept of the "buried self" as a reliable substantiality, Arnold tried to come to terms with emerging problems and thereby to achieve a self-possession. As he wrote to his confidant, Clough, he wanted "*a distinct feeling of [his] way as far as [his] own nature is concerned* " (emphases added, Culler 552).

Though partly supported by Arnold's own remark, Honan's exclusively biographical approach to the poem, however informative, has the danger of degenerating Arnold's poems into a record of growing pains. Arnold's search for the "buried self," then, might be interpreted as nothing but his retrogressive and vain longing for a return to the pre – adolescent stage of life in which one's identity is established through one's merging with surroundings, in Arnold's case, with his sister, brother, and his friends. Furthermore, Honan's rather sympathetic association of Arnold's personal sense of loss with his search for the "buried life" as a supplementary value cannot fully explain his incessant passion for the "buried life." For the same theme appears recurrently in several of his poems, with the "buried life" as a motif, either explicit or implied.

In Arnold's poems, the idea of the "buried self" seems to exceed a metaphorical means of reconciling the poet with his personal dilemma. It goes beyond the personal level and signifies something archetypal and social, so much so that often the man Matthew's personal sense of loss can be seen as a metonymy of that of the period itself caught by the poet Arnold. Even his nostalgia for an exceptionally close relationship with family members and friends might refer to an earlier environment in which one could see life unfolded with its unified purpose. For as Miller points out, essential to Arnold's nostalgia for the past is directed to an epoch of harmony in which the "idea of fusion, of intimacy, and of participation" (216) is dominant.

As an epitome of Arnold's strenuous efforts for authority, his concept of the "buried self" both expresses and records the process by which a happy past is overcome by the melancholy present, Romantic notion of the self is disintegrated and its existential notion emerges, and a God-centered world is replaced with a de-centered universe. In the same way as the Romantic poets take creative imagination and the self as "the center of defence against the disintegrating tendencies of the age" (Williams 280), Arnold tries to find a remedy, albeit an emergency measure, in his grasp of the "buried self."

Arnold's somewhat weighty approach to the subject against the rather personal and light poetic situation supports such an interpretation. In the speaker's general theorizing after the first stanza, one becomes suspicious of the confessional quality of the poem and aware that the "buried life" is meant to enter into a universal, archetypal realm of human experience, giving validity to the poet's search for it. Then, his presentation of the lovers as main witnesses of the "buried life" has significance only in that they form the basic unit of society. Arnold does not seem to consider the love relationship so much for its face value as for being a proper paradigm of society.

Arnold's manipulation of the narrative further supports such a conjecture. After the first stanza, the extremely subjective "I" is shifted to a representational "we," and to a more objectified form "he." Being consistent with it, the conversational tone of the first stanza yields to an objective, speculative, and a sort of internal monologue mode. Such a polyphonic adoption of the poetic voice effects a display of the multi-facets of the "buried life." Though subtle, the "buried life" goes beyond an infrequent emergence from the substratum of an individual's existence: it becomes a basis for an "aesthetic of generality," whereby Arnold seeks out a motif for the "perfection" that "appeals to the most universal human passions" (Chris 34). It is acknowledged not as a mere counterpart of an individual's "social self" or "public self," but as the "*same heart that beats in every human breast*" (emphasis added). Arnold's quasi-mystical apprehension of the "buried life" is analogous to such a concept as Jung's collective unconscious or Plato's Idea.

Though coherent with modern psychology in his interest in the subconscious, or unconscious, Arnold departs from it in his "reject[ion] of the division of man's nature into multiple faculties" (Miller 225), as was seen in Jung's division of archetypes into "animus and anima, and persona and shadow" (*The Encyclopedia of Philosophy*, Vol. 4, 295). Instead, being a self-proclaimed transcendentalist, Arnold was so much influenced by Emerson's notion of Over-Soul that his notion of the "buried self" seems to be the poetic exposition of Emersonian "Over-Soul," though veered more to the existential condition of human beings. Based upon Emersonian notion that "man is a stream whose source is hidden" (Bradley 628), Arnold establishes a notion that "each man is inwardly and secretly one, as coral islands, separate on the surface, are joined in the deeps" (Miller 225). He had a firm belief that, if the world external to a human being is a part of the unity hidden behind, then it would be possible to reach that unity by tracing any one of the separate elements back. He thus affirms the possession of the "unregarded river of our life" is the same as getting simultaneously the hills where life rose/And the sea where it goes."

Arnold's archetypal grasp of the "buried life" enriches its implications as the speaker's speculation proceeds. Its meaning becomes more comprehensive and its influence farther – reaching. As an all – inclusive term, the scope of the "buried life" ranges from the very origin to the ultimate end of human existence, only through the understanding of which are we able to know "whence our lives come and where they go" (l. 54). Metaphysically, it becomes "the unalienable law of his being, a law which is at once within him and outside him" (Miller 231). This makes him break allegiances with the physical world, and drives him on toward a hidden goal. When he reaches this goal, he will recover his "genuine self," and at the same time regain the intimacy with all things lost. Almost equivalent to something like an absolute principle of existence or the primal law of being, the "buried life" contributes to a realm of knowledge that belongs to God, a sure foundation of poetic creativity.

In Arnold's creative activity, this poem marks a turning point in its mode of expression: it registers his transition from poetry to prose. In the speaker's attitude toward the poetic subject and the manipulation of the tone and of the relationship between the speaker and the listener, the poem is divided into two parts: the first stanza on the one hand, and the remainder of the poem, on the other. In the first stanza, the speaker's articulation is directed to his lover, whereas in the rest of the poem, it is directed to the reader in general. The tone is also changed by the relationship between the speaker and his listener. If the first stanza is characterized by the speaker's sadness for the incommunicability between lovers, the rest of the poem is marked by the speaker's commentary or prosaic exposition of the previous scene. Whereas there is the 'here and now' poetic situation in the first stanza, the rest of the poem hinges on timelessness or un-time consciousness of the speaker. Because of the fragmentary quality of the poetic situation, there is no explicit poetic action going on based upon the relationship of the poetic elements in the latter part. The second part does not show any movement: it remains static and stagnant within the speaker's consciousness.

The static non-movement of the poetic situation intensifies the infertility of love. The apparent love poem records, instead of the expected consumate love, the speaker's anxiety about and desperate search for the "buried self," the possible commonground that would connect the lovers. The speaker's flowing eloquence at the beginning of the poem is nothing but a camouflage that is employed to conceal, but more explicitly reveal, the lack of communicability as well as difficulty of the conceptualization of the "buried life."

Nevertheless, the very claim that the "buried life" can be the common binding element of all human beings shows how one can have access to and retrieve it: that is, to trace back the elements to the origin. In the last two stanzas, Arnold illustrates the "rare moments" in which one attains a "heightened vision" (Stange 175) of the "buried life":

> Only − but this is rare −
> When a beloved hand is laid in ours,
> When, jaded with the rush and glare
> Of the interminable hours,
> Our eyes can in another's eyes read clear,
> When our world-deafen'd ear
> Is by the tones of a loved voice caress'd −
> A bolt is shot back somewhere in our breast,
> And a lost pulse of feeling stirs again.
> The eye sinks inward, and the heart lies plain,
> And what we mean, we say, and what we would, we know.
> A man becomes aware of his life's flow,
> And hears its winding murmur. and he sees
> The meadows where it glides, the sun, the breeze.
>
> And there arrives a lull in the hot race
> Wherein he doth for ever chase
> That flying and elusive shadow, rest.
> An air or coolness plays upon his face,
> And an unwonted calm pervades his breast.
> And then he thinks he knows
> The hills where his life rose,
> And the sea where it goes. (ll. 77-98).

It is only through one's sharing experience with other human beings, even "not 'in' love, but 'through' love" (Stange 175), that one reconfirms the effect of the "buried life": "he thinks he knows/The hills where his life rose,/And the sea where it goes." Only by sharing the inmost soul with the beloved can one recover a "lost pulse of feeling," "become aware of his life's flow" and achieve a true communication: "[A]nd what we mean, we say, and what we would, we know." Love here is exhibited as the main agent of the "buried life," and not an ultimate end. And this explains why the poem does not dramatize the celebration of consummate love, but regulates the "buried life" in terms of its communal value.

The inherent social quality of the "buried life," as an important signifier of what Arnold pursues as a thematic center of his poetry, explains though partly, the reason why Arnold had to delete his poem, "Empedocles on Etna" from his 1852 collection of poems. Perhaps, as Carol Christi points out, he suppressed it "because of the unrelieved painfulness, which resulted from Empedocles's isolation in his self-consciousness with no vent for his suffering in action" (34), or, as Arnold explains it, "the dialogue of the mind with itself," far from offering exciting new possibilities of experience, becomes a prison which isolates Empedocles on top of the mountain. But considering Arnold's keen sensitivity to the social quality of the "buried self," one can easily conclude that Empedocles's self – declamation of his relationship with God and other human beings could not help Arnold's discarding this excessively romantic poem in that volume. Empedocles' wrong approach to the "buried self" by isolating himself from human society is too incompatible with the nature of the "buried self."

In spite of its social characteristics, "the buried self," exposed to human society, is thwarted, suppressed, and hidden, either by various social impositions, or by individual's wilful choice. On the one hand, in the form of a fable, Arnold attributes the burial of "the genuine self" to "Fate" whose precarious anxiety keeps it away from one's "frivolous" disposition: "Fate, which foresaw/How frivolous a baby man would be − ⋯ it might keep from his capricious play/His genuine self,⋯" (ll. 30-37). On the other hand, Arnold does not ignore that this banishment of the "buried self" is done by "our own call" (l. 71): he makes it clear that we tend to deliberately ignore or renounce its existence for fear of "melancholy[which the 'buried self' brings] into all our day" (l. 76) and thus, threatens our superficially complacent life.

In consequence, an "unfathomable inner gulf" (Stange 174) is built between one's true self and one's social self or external self. For the first time in human history, Victorians realized that each person was not only "alien to the rest/Of men, [but also] alien to themselves" (ll. 21-22), residing "in the sea of life enisled" ("To Marguerite − Continued," l. 1). In the extreme separation, these two selves are grafted to two different social classes, their fixation as Somerset Maugham satirizes in his book, *The Summing Up,*

> The celebrated develops a technique to deal with persons they come across. They show the world a mask, often an impressive one, but take care to conceal their real selves. They play the part that is expected from them and with practice learn to play it very well, but you are stupid if you think that this public performance of theirs corresponds with the man within ⋯⋯ I have been more concerned with the obscure than with the famous. They are more often themselves. They have had no need to create a figure to protect themselves from the world or

to impress it. (pp. 7-8).

The filling of the gap between the two selves is as hard and unrealistic as the annihilation of social classes. It is not achieved merely by one's vague and wishful yearning for "buried self" either. For its emergence is so infrequent, so unpredictable, and so arbitrary that it is not easily within our grasp.

The tragic sense that one cannot completely reach the "buried self" lurks even in the epiphanic moment of love (ll. 77-98). Although one gets reaffirmation of the existence of the buried self through love, it is "rare" and no more than a "rest" from a "flying and elusive shadow" (l. 93). This epiphanic experience includes itself an anti-epiphanic moment. One can get fragmentary glimpses, a few facets of the whole, but never the whole. It does not guarantee a sustaining stay.

Moreover, when we consider that the blissful moment cannot be embodied as a living experience of the narrator himself, this tragic sense is intensified. The man who participates in this "rare" moment is not "I" of the first section, but "he," a somebody who had the luck to witness the "buried self." Arnold, not to mention the narrator, is an outsider excluded from this realization. Insofar as the "buried self" is concerned, Arnold, the narrator, and even the reader still remain uncertain and dissatisfied.

The unsatisfactory experience with the "buried life" and the very difficulty in defining its reality often drives Arnoldian characters back to a "wandering between two desires··· One drives to the world without,/And one to solitude" ("Stanzas in Memory of the Author of 'Oberman'," ll.

93-96). The very affirmation, however, that there is something that is termed the "buried life" makes it hard to give up our quest and makes us commit ourselves to the world of action. The inclination to search for the "buried life" outweighs one's conscious commitment to "many thousand lines" (l. 57) of "nothing" (l. 69).

Arnold's suggestion of a life of resignation as well as of 'self-dependence' is just an aspect of his irresistible inclination toward such search for the "buried life" through passive preservation of that self. By keeping oneself aloof from society, and by repudiating the false selves which have engulfed him in the rush and hurry of urban life, he can at least prevent further sacrifice and contamination of the genuine self by social impositions including multitudinous role-play. By virtue of its utmost purity, the buried genuine self, once exposed to society, will soon be contaminated and corrupted – more easily than the 'ordinary self.' Furthermore, one can, at best, retrieves the already – lost portion of his "buried self" and nourish it, so that it contributes to ameliorate man's life and furthers human evolution.

Such a yearning to preserve the integrity of his "buried life," to keep the "sad lucidity of the soul," to live a life of resignation is linked to Arnold's definition and role of the poet. In another poem, "Resignation," Arnold presents a viable case for a life of resignation. Grouping men by their modes of living – such as the activist pilgrims, the wise men who have achieved resignation, the Faustian sensationalists, and the gypsies – Arnold presents himself as an aspirant to the life of resignation. As a model of "the highest form of resignation" (Stange 61), Arnold portrays the wise bard who has, by "schooling of the stubborn mind," by labor, and by suffering, "achieved the which a thoughtful and serious writer might aspire" (Stange 62). And this "wise bard," embodied in three figures – Homer, Epictetus, and Sophocles – becomes Arnold's "prop" ("To a Friend," l. 1), a model to follow.

The most characteristic aspect of a life of resignation is one's disinterested attitude toward areas of human experience. The primary yardstick of the poet's greatness is his "disinterested view" of life and the world. This "disinterestedness," a core of Arnoldian critical spirit, does not indicate one's indifference to or ignorance of the practical world of reality. Neither is it an escapist tendency. It is instead a free stance, or, an austerely objective attitude toward life and the world. Only through a "free play of mind" ("The Function of the Criticism at the Present Time," 247) from the detached stance, can the poet do the world any service.

Such resignation of the poet enables him to accommodate human experience into the total vision of life, because a life of resignation and the ability to hold a holistic view of the world are in mutual dependence. Since he is resigned from social involvement, the poet is able to see "life unroll,/A placid and continuous whole – /That general life···" (ll. 189-192).

Conversely, in order to see the world in totality, the poet's distance and detachment from society is prerequisite.

Such a holistic vision achieved by the poet's resignation is assimilated into the "buried life" in the last part of the poem "Empedocles on Etna." Before he plunges into the crater of the volcano, Empedocles speculates on the possibility of an after – life. Measuring the probability of reincarnation after death, Empedocles suggests that our life in this world is only a "test of our fidelity to the inner life" (Stange 181):

Go through the sad probation all again,
To see if we will poise our life at last,
To see if we still now at last be true
To our own only true, deep –buried selves,

Being one with which we are one with the whole world.

(emphases added, ll. 368-372).

Not only does the "buried life" provide a reservoir of power which one ceaselessly turns to but it also functions as an instrument of a person's participation into the "whole world." Only through one's recovery of the "buried self" can one get a total vision of the world and join that world as a legitimate member. Then one will possess God, and subsequently one's true self which one has since lost, and vice versa, and possessing the true self, one can possess God again who was vanished. And in this process, the function of love, described in terms of its sensual appeal and erotic quality, turns out to be an agent or a bringer of "the buried self" as was quoted before:

When a beloved hand is laid in ours,
When ⋯
Our eyes can in another's eyes read clear,
When our world-deafen'd ear
Is by the tones of a loved voice caress'd – (ll. 78-83).

Once confirmed, the "buried life" exerts a powerful influence upon one's view of himself and of the world. One can depend on one's "buried self" and in order to reach it one can spend one's whole life – time without any regret, just like the visionary Poet in Shelley's poem, "Alastor." Then, one can locate the reservoir of power in oneself: One hears, "Resolve to be thyself; and know that he,/Who finds himself, loses his misery" ("Self – Dependence," ll. 31-32). The very affirmation that we have our buried selves somewhere in us thus becomes a sustaining power to continue our quest and to view life as a worthwhile effort.

Arnold's confidence of his existence and the immense potentiality of the "buried self" leads him to a philosophy of "self-dependence," something similar to Emerson's 'self-reliance.' In fact, the notion of the "buried self" provides a deep structure of his notion of culture. Upon a solid base of the "buried self" Arnold maintains, one should pursue perfection:

> ⋯⋯ perfection, and of harmonious perfection, general perfection and perfection which consists in becoming something rather than in having something, in an inward condition of the mind and spirit, not in an outward set of circumstances. ("Culture and Anarchy," 413).

With the "buried life" in the center, as a thesis of Arnold's literary activity, the coherence and unity of his works become clear. Though divided into two genres, his creative aim was one, that is, to find a remedy for the illnesses of the period, and both his poetry and prose greatly contribute to this task. If he seeks for the identity of the "buried self" through his poetry, he activates, in his prose writings, the affirmed notion and establishes more sophisticated concepts with it as a basis. Likewise, if, through his poetry, he diagnoses the illnesses of the time – "with its sick hurry, its divided aims,/Its head o'er taxed, its palsied hearts" ("The Scholar – Gipsy," ll. 204-05) –

through his prose writings, he prescribes at least some "anodyne" for those symptoms in terms of culture and further humanism. Even what Arnold suggests as the central sub-concepts of culture, those of "sweetness and lightness" seem to be the "buried life" retrieved, which transforms one's 'ordinary self' into 'the best self.'

The final appeal of Arnold's pursuit of the "buried self" rests on his strong confidence in its existence. And what decides the success or failure of such effort is the poet's belief and not his knowledge. In a society in which faith lent its power to scepticism and scientific agnosticism, Arnold presents a strong case for having faith and what it means to an individual. And in such a process, his concept of "the buried self" evolves as the central self in his creative imagination, and his poem "The Buried Life" forms an integral part.

< Works Cited >

Bradley, Sculley, et al. Edit. *American Tradition in Literature*. New York: A. W. W. Norton Book, 1967.

Buckley, J. H. *The Victorian Temper*. Cambridge, Mass. : Harvard Univ. Press, 1951.

Christ, Carol. *The Finer Optic*. New Haven & London: Yale Univ. Press, 1975.

Culler, A. Dwight. Edit. *Poetry and Criticism of Matthew Arnold*. Arnold. Boston: Houghton Mifflin Co, 1961.

Honan, Park. *Matthew Arnold: A Life*. New York: McGraw Hill Book Co; 1981.

Hough, Graham. *The Last Romantics*. London: Metheun, NY: Barnes & Noble, 1961.

Maugham, W. Somerset. *The Summing Up*. A Mentor Book, Pub. by the New American Library, 1938.

Miller, J. Hillis. *The Disappearance of God*. Cambridge: The Belknap Press of Harvard Univ. Press, 1963.

Stange, G. Robert. *Matthew Arnold: The Poet as Humanist*. Princeton, New Jersey: Princeton Univ. Press, 1967.

Sypher, Wylie. *Loss of the Self in Modern Literature and Art*. Vintage Books, NY: Random House, 1962.

Williams, Raymond. "The Romantic Artist," *Romanticism: Points of View*. Ed. by Robert F. Gleckner & G. E. Enscoe. Detroit: Wayne Univ. Press, 1975.

II - 2. The Creation of A Female Myth: A Study on Christina Rossetti's "Goblin Market"

Critical reception of Christina Rossetti's most significant narrative poem, "Goblin Market" (1859) has been varied, "endlessly susceptible to new interpretations" (Cosslett 19). With its elements of fantasy, fairy tale, social commentary, sexual undertones, and religious hermeneutics, all mixing together and jostling against one another, this poem has shown itself to tread "a breathtakingly thin line between nursery rhyme, sexual fantasy, religious allegory and social criticism" (Leighton 135), consequently, providing compelling dynamics and poetic energy.

As the critical response of the poem has been diverse, so has been the interpretation of the relationship between the two sisters, Laura and Lizzie. Being depicted variously as "Freudian children, figural types, practicing lesbians, and as 'sisters' in the feminist sense" (Bentley 57), they have been subject to consistent controversy in their poetic roles. Dorothy Mermin focuses on Lizzie's heroic exploit and argues that Lizzie is the true heroine, bringing redemption to her curious and helpless sister Laura who faces imminent death. She claims that the poem commemorates sisterly love in its power of salvation and life-giving influence represented by the heroine Lizzie's sacrificial love, thus elevating her role to be the only feminine hero that counts. Behind such claim lies a rather concessive presupposition – Laura, a trouble maker, is considered to be a passive and receptive figure throughout, an object waiting to be cared for and saved by her sister Lizzie.

Sandra Gilbert & Susan Gubar, while raising Lizzie's role to that of "a female savior" (566), turn fresh attention on Laura and place her at the center of the poetic argument. In their land mark study of Victorian women poets, entitled *Madwoman in the Attic*, Gilbert and Gubar read Laura's fall and regeneration in terms of emergence of a woman poet in the male-dominant literary world of the Nineteenth – Century England. Identifying Laura with a female writer, they juxtapose the story of redemption to a parallel scheme dealing with the emergence of a repressive woman poet who "wishes to experience the full fruits of her imagination, but too much bounded by convention, is unable to have this freedom" (Maxwell 80) and should work with 'the aesthetics of renunciation.' Though significant in their effort to trace the psychology of a female poet in the rather hostile world of creation, their reading stresses her subdued situation, thus unable to accommodate the commemorative tone in the last part of the poem in which Laura celebrates the value of sisterly love.

Gerome McGann develops these two positions into a dialectical reading of the roles of the two sisters. In his reading, the two sisters take equally important roles in the development of the story of redemption:

> So far as "Goblin Market" tells a story of 'redemption,' the process is carried out in the dialectic of the acts of both Laura and Lizzie··· The definitive sign of their dialectical relationship appears in the simple fact that Laura is not finally victimized. She is only a victim as Jesus is a victim; she is a suffering servant. In a very real sense, therefore, the poem represents Laura as the moral begetter of Lizzie. Lizzie does not 'save' Laura. Both together enact a drama which displays what moral forces have to be exerted in order, not to be saved from evil.

but simply to grow up (108).

Although McGann's eclectic reading offers a balanced view of the previous two positions, his comprehension of Laura shows significant lack of coherence: while he exaggerates Laura's status to be a victim in the same way "as Jesus is a victim," he is unable to understand Laura's change as a main element securing her redemption. His view seems legitimate in so far as he considers Laura's succumbing to temptation and the consequent fall as the very cause and motif of Lizzie's sacrificial adventure, but his failure to comprehend Laura's role in her own regeneration produces only a limited interpretation of the poetic action.

Correcting the two opposite views on the roles of the two sisters in "Goblin Market" and complementing McGann's insufficient coverage of Laura's role, this paper aims at illuminating two aspects of the poem. The first one is related to a more fundamental and religious question regarding the nature of redemption. It can be phrased: Can anyone be redeemed by another person without any effort by one's self? The second point deals with the validity of the poetic ending. Scholars who consider Lizzie only as the poetic heroine do not provide a satisfactory explanation of the reason for Laura's receiving so much attention at the end of the poem, where she carries its main message, i. e. the values of sisterly love and sacrifice. This second question, being pertinent to the coherence of the poetic plot, revolves around a couple of specific questions: How can we explain the sudden highlighting of Laura at the end of the poem?; To what extent can we endow Laura with the quality of a feminist hero, if she deserves such a major role?; How to reconcile the seemingly inconsistent narrative between the last part and the rest of the poem?

With such aims in mind, this paper traces the process the two poetic heroines undergo in overcoming difficulties and temptations to finally find the answers to the age-old but, at the same time, most urgent question 'how to live as women in a male-dominant world which is hostile to them?' A close look at both the text and poetic metaphor illuminates that the characters, particularly Laura, go through a substantial change in their understanding and attitude toward others. Considering Laura has remained a relatively obscure figure in Rossetti's criticism up until Gilbert & Gubar, one expected result is to shed light on the validity of her experience and further elevate her role to that of a feminist hero, hopefully as important as, or even more important than Lizzie. Such a reading will support the premise that a seemingly – sudden highlighting of Laura's role in the last part of the poem is not so abrupt or groundless after all, but rather based on a dramatic, but altruistic change in Laura herself.

To a certain extent, all literary works presuppose the characters' change, and it is no exception with Rossetti's characters in her epic-narrative, "Goblin Market." As a story of redemption, this poem portrays the change of poetic characters and records their mental/spiritual growth in a way that qualifies them as literary hero (in)es. The main action of the poem incorporates Laura's experience. Roughly, it follows a rather stereotypical rites – of – passage – pattern conventionally described in literature: Laura, an innocent maiden succumbs to goblin men's temptations; she suffers from a death – in – life experience of her fall; Lizzie, her sympathetic sister, ventures to find the solution; much moved Laura is changed, rewarded with redemption and enjoys a happy domestic life in the end. Quite clearly, it is Laura's experience which is "central and decisive" (Edmond 200). On the surface, the poem features a situation in which Laura, by tasting the forbidden fruit, opens the way for the necessity of her redemption and which anticipates the poem's vision of sisterhood (Edmond 182). On a more spiritual level, the movement of the poem is towards Laura's recognition that what she has desired is really "wormwood to her tongue," a costly realization of the limitations of the goblin men's fruit. Lizzie's role, though crucial, is responsive and focused on countermeasures to solve an already – existing problem. Although Lizzie initiates Laura's redemptive process, it is the change of the fallen character Laura that preconditions her own regeneration.

In a more extended context, Laura's role is elevated to that of a female hero who, with the help of her heroic sister Lizzie, comes to grips with the important communal truth, i. e. only through sisterly love can women save themselves and gain proper social positions and roles. In its social implications, this poem marks Rossetti's challenge to male-oriented Victorian society and provides a viable alternative through the cooperative efforts of the sisters.

Such a reading puts the poem on a par with the acclaimed myths and legends of many male-dominant cultures, which Campbell delineates in his noted work, *The Hero With A Thousand Faces*. Campbell describes the pattern a mythological hero follows in his journey:

The standard path of the mythological adventure of the hero is a magnification of the formula represented in the rites of the passage: separation[temptation] – initiation[fall] – return[regeneration]: which might be named the nuclear unit of the mono-myth.

A hero ventures forth from the world of common day into a region of supernatural wonder: fabulous forces are there encountered and a decisive victory is won: the hero comes back with the power to bestow boons on his fellow man (30).

Though mainly psychological and not strictly consistent with the steps heroes take in their journey, Laura and Lizzie's action/situation makes a parallel contour with that of the mythical hero and helps locate the poem at the center of the famous mythical and legendary stories of the world.

1. Separation (or, Temptation):

In his afore-mentioned study on myth, Campbell illustrates how a hero/heroine unknowingly enters into a world of adventure that drastically changes his/her fate. Just like the Princess in the fable, "Frog Prince," Laura and Lizzie, two ordinary modern female heroes are innocently caught up in the fruit-bearers' cry for the sale of the fruit. The chance meeting throws the sisters headlong into a long and difficult journey that leads them to important knowledge about themselves and those around them.

The first part of the poem draws special attention to Rossetti's accurate examination into the nature and effect of the temptation. First, Rossetti describes the temptation in terms of its irresistible power: the fruit vendors' cry, with its sensual appeal and almost mesmeric sound effect, creates a strong hypnotic world of temptation which draws in not only the two sisters but also the readers:

> Morning and evening
> Maids heard the goblins cry:
> 'Come buy our orchard fruits,
> Come buy, come buy:
> Apples and quinces,
> ......
> All ripe together
> In summer weather,
> Morns that pass by,
> Fair eves that fly;
> Come buy, come buy:
> Our grapes fresh from the vine,
> ......
> Taste them and try:
> Currants and gooseberries,
> Bright − fire − like barberries,
> Figs to fill your mouth,
> Citrons from the South,
> Sweet to tongue and sound to eye;
> Come buy, come buy.' (ll. 1-31)

Noticeable in this luxuriant inventory of exotic fruits is Rossetti's dexterity with which she inserts the goblin men's incremental tactics to entice the sisters. It shows how gradually but firmly the temptation builds its hold on Laura and Lizzie: reinforced by the refrain "come buy, come buy," it moves from a general introduction in "All ripe together/In summer weather, – " (ll.14-15) to a straightforward invitation in "Taste them and try" (l. 25), culminating in persuasive reasoning reminiscent of Eve and the fruit of the tree of knowledge which looked "Sweet to tongue and sound to eye" (l. 30). The goblin men's cry to sell the fruit appears to be a modern day "call to adventure" (Campbell 49), and with that Laura is drawn into a dangerous relationship with negative forces which are "odd," "queer," and "unnatural."

By emphasizing the irresistible quality of the temptation, Rossetti seems to be preparing an excuse for Laura's fall. Indeed, nowhere in the poem is the description of Laura and her precipitous act condemnatory. As Edmond rightly points out, "there is nothing unsympathetic in the presentation of Laura's character" (200). In the cautionary moral tale, she would be 'foolish Laura' or 'vulnerable Laura' who is self-indulgent, egocentric and lacking in will-power; in this poem, however, "there is nothing more severe or less ambiguous than 'sweet-tooth' Laura." (Edmond 200). The narrator maintains a sympathetic tone throughout. By turning Laura's surrender to temptation into an inevitable conclusion, Rossetti brings the whole pattern of the poetic experience within the paradigm of the heroes' journey as described by Campbell.

As interesting as the temptation is, the process in which Laura succumbs to temptation is even more so, showing a delicate play of mind which ranges from stern refusals, hesitations and psychological fluctuations, and illusory distortions concerning the true nature of the fruit. When she at first "hear[s]" the goblin men's cry for the sale of the fantastic fruit, Laura, just like Lizzie, is timid and reluctant and thrusts herself back to the premonition she had learned from adults. On the surface, Laura's attitude displays no difference from the typical reaction any maiden would show when confronted with an unfamiliar event:

> We must not look at goblin men,
> We must not buy their fruits:
> Who knows upon what soil they fed
> Their hungry thirsty roots? (ll. 42-45)

With its smooth flow and almost mechanical rhythm, the same passage, however, carries the undertone of a ready-made formula, a stereotypical first-hand response with a verbatim quotation from the adults. Her suspicion of the origin of the fruit has, in particular, an overtone of affectation or a reflection of knowledge imposed by or borrowed from adults. Paradoxically, Laura's recitation of such imposed warning itself signals her turn away from conventional wisdom, and from Lizzie, an emblem of self-control and reason, and a devoted keeper of the lessons.

In sharp contrast to Lizzie's constant resistance, Laura's impulsive and rash temperament makes her an easy prey to desire. The conflict Laura experiences between curiosity and moral responsibility ends up with her curiosity prevailing. Preoccupied with a strong desire for the forbidden fruit, Laura justifies her action by escaping to a world of illusory imagination. As a "sign of the impairment of Laura's reasoning abilities" (Bentley 68), this shows a pathetic self-deceit:

How fair the vine must grow
Whose grapes are so luscious;
How warm the wind must blow
Through those fruit bushes. (ll. 60-64)

In the same way, in the nick of her surrender to temptation, she transfers
the evil goblin men into kind benefactors with "a voice like voice of doves"
which "sounded kind and full of loves/In the pleasant weather" (ll. 77-80).

Again, Rossetti takes great care not to take an 'upbraiding' tone when
describing Laura's rash behavior. It is highly likely that from the onset of
the poetic action, Rossetti is careful not to convey any negative implication
of Laura's yielding to temptation. It becomes quite evident in her use of
similes. She describes Laura's allured attitude through her gleaming neck
and compares it to "a rush-imbedded swan," "a lily from the beck," "a
moonlit poplar branch," and most effectively "a vessel at the launch/When
its last restraint is gone" (ll. 82-86). In contrast to the seriousness of the
tone implied in the premonition, the employed images are light, romantic,
and beautiful, far from carrying negative overtones. They are either
expressive of Laura's innocence and beauty as in "a swan," "a lily," and "a
moonlit poplar branch" or of the freedom and energy Laura might have felt
as "a vessel at the launch/When its last restraint is gone."

Rossetti's ambiguous treatment of Laura has the danger of undermining
the violence and cruelty of the goblin men. But Rossetti's intention seems to
be clear: by not using obviously disapproving similes, she shows not only her
sympathy for Laura, but also indicates that the journey Laura has to make –
which is predominantly psychological and sexual – is imperative for her

growth. Likewise, by featuring Laura's fall in terms of inevitability and vulnerability, Rossetti seems to justify Laura's narrative-dominance at the end of the poem. From a purely positive aspect, the goblin men's seduction initiates Laura's long and tormented journey which, nevertheless, becomes essential to her growth.

2. Initiation (or, the Fall):

Laura's venture shares several elements of danger and hardship with the ones male heroes undergo in their quests described by Campbell. The first such obstacle Laura faces is, however, more realistic than those of other heroes: "Laura stared but did not stir,/Longed but had no money" (ll.105-106). Such a gap between Laura's desire and her financial inability further predicts her moral incapacity to take responsibility for her choice, introducing at the same time, another important motif of the female body being degraded into a commodity in a capitalistic market system. A clear indication of Rossetti's criticism of emerging capitalism, such a gap corners Laura into no choice but to sell a part of her body, her golden hair, to purchase the forbidden fruit.

> "Buy from us with a golden curl."
> She clipped a precious golden lock,
> She dropped a tear more rare than pearl,
> Then sucked their fruit globes fair or red:
> Sweeter than honey from the rock,

Stronger than man – rejoicing wine,
Clearer than water flowed that juice; (ll. 125-131)

In substituting a "precious" (l. 126) part of herself for the lack of money, Laura accedes to "a process of dehumanization and commercialization whereby she becomes simultaneously a buyer and a seller, a consumer and a commodity" (Bentley 70). Helsinger, in her article entitled "Consumer Power & the Utopia of Desire: Christina Rossetti's *Goblin Market*" connects the collapse of a self – sufficient economy and the emergence of a mercantile market system to the further deterioration of the already-helpless women in the Nineteenth – Century England. By featuring Laura as the victim of the emerging mercantile economy, Rossetti places Laura's individual misfortune in a more extended social context, further raising Laura's problem to a collective issue of all women in Victorian society and preparing at the same time the need for another woman Lizzie's intercession in the plot.

The second, more formidable danger of the temptation is an inherent one. Represented by a gap between expectation and reality, the fruit, once tasted, causes an unquenchable thirst instead of satisfying Laura's desire. As its insatiability grows, so does Laura's illusion of the fruit increase until finally Laura indulges in a false fantasy of the fruits: cherries "fresh on their mother-twigs," "icy-cold" melons, peaches "with a velvet nap," and "pellucid grapes without one seed" and "with sugar – sweet" sap (ll. 171-183).

On analysis, Laura's fall is caused by her misunderstanding of the nature of the fruit as the object of desire, i. e. a maiden can have only one chance to buy it. In the poem, after one transaction with the goblin men, Laura is not able to hear them again: "Listening ever, but not catching./The customary cry,/Come buy, come buy" (ll. 230-232). Such once-and-for-all opportunity has raised constant controversy concerning the nature of experience Laura goes through. Scholars including Brownley argue that the main poetic experience embodies "a feminine initiation into adult sexuality" (179) ranging from the loss of virginity through initiation of adult sexuality and to marriage. Though partly true, such one-sided reading does not incorporate the multi-layered elements of economy, religion, fantasy, and social criticism which Rossetti proposes. It has the danger of narrowing the scope of the poetic experience. Rather than being exclusively sexual, the poem deals with broader issues of innocence and experience involved in a maiden's rite-of-passage. Just as Campbell's mythical/legendary heroes undergo extreme testing period replete with dangers, risks, and violence, Laura also goes through a devastating experience characterized by the disarray of her existent lifestyle, depression, anorexia, and general loss of life's vitality. Worse, Laura becomes a victim of self-pity who refuses to share her pain with others. Anxiously longing for the fruit, she isolates herself not only from ordinary life, but also from her sister Lizzie. Laura in her self-imprisonment recalls helpless mythical heroes who, stuck in the 'Chapel Perilous,' are unable to carry out the assigned missions:

"She said not one word in her heart's sore ache;
...
So crept to bed, and lay

Silent till Lizzie slept;
Then sat up in a passionate yearning,
And gnashed her teeth for baulked desire, and wept
As if her heart would break. (ll. 261-268)

Reminding one of the vegetation myth in which the king's illness causes national disaster, Laura's personal devastation is expanded into the barrenness and infertility of the area around her and into the realm of nature. The seeds she sowed have not sprouted, her "tree of life drooped from the root" (l. 260), and she experiences a near death – in – life experience: "dwindling/[she] Seemed knocking at Death's door" (ll. 320-321). Laura follows the exact path Jeannie had undergone before she died: she is on the point of repeating the same fatal mistake as Jeannie, her tragic precursor, did.

3. Return (or, Regeneration)

Laura's fate begins to take a turn for the better with the intrusion of Lizzie who assumes the role of problem-solver, without the supernatural powers present in the traditional version of the hero's tale. Despite her lack of supernatural powers or maybe because of this, Lizzie renders a sense of reality, adding plausibility to the plot. Her potential to play such an important role in Laura's life lies embedded in their similitude:

Golden head by golden head,

> Like two pigeons in one nest
> Folded in each other's wings,
> They lay down in their curtained bed:
> Like two blossoms on one stem,
> Like two flakes of new-fall'n snow,
> Like two wands of ivory
> Tipped with gold for awful kings.
> Moon and stars gazed in at them,
> Wind sang to them lullaby,
> Lumbering owls forbore to fly,
> Not a bat flapped to and fro
> Round in their nest:
> Cheek to cheek and breast to breast
> Locked together in one nest. (ll. 184-198)

This scene, drawn immediately after Laura has eaten the fruit, suggests that the relationship between the sisters be persistent and on-going, regardless of one's sinfulness. Laura and Lizzie are presented here not only as alter – egos of each other, but also as together belonging to the world of nature, following its rhythm. Under the protection of nature, the sisters' solidarity and kinship is firmly secured. This scene, directly connected to the morning scene in which Laura is wakened "laugh[ing] in the innocent old way" (l. 538), predicts Laura and Lizzie's return to the world of nature.

If Laura's suffering is intensified because of her inability to hear the goblin's cry, Lizzie's role as a 'boom – bringer' is facilitated by her ability to hear it, and by her easy accessibility to the fruit. But above all, it is Lizzie's will that endows her with such a role: she is willing to sacrifice herself for her sister. Unable to "bear/To watch her sister's cankerous care/Yet not to share" (ll. 299-301), "tender" Lizzie "*weighed no more /Better and worse*" but, "for the first time in her life/Began to listen and look" (ll. 322-323 & 327-328, emphases added). A comparison of Lizzie's attitude before and after her decision to "buy fruit to comfort [Laura]" (l. 310) makes it clear that Lizzie transforms herself from a reserved, calculating maiden – who "feared to pay too dear" (l. 311) – to a willing victim of self – sacrificial love – who "weighed no more." Lizzie's determination implied in the latter reveals the intensity of her sisterly love and the danger her adventure entails.

The trial Lizzie goes through takes the form of sexual harrassment which involves reckless abuse, insults, and physical violence. Lizzie is physically hurt and injured, but when the goblins were "[w]orn out by her resistance and flung back her penny" (ll. 438-439) and vanished, her mind was glad, the bounce of returned coins sounded "music to her ear" (l. 454), and she achieves moral and psychological victory over the goblins. As D'Amico maintains, Lizzie's successful confrontation with the goblin men "marks a stage in her spiritual development" (74), culminating in the ensuing scene of Christian Eucharist in which she becomes a figure of Christ himself.

It is at this scene of communion that Rossetti's attack on the male – dominant tone of the Bible and the Christian view of original sin reaches its climax. First, by featuring Lizzie as an evolved female Adam in her effort to rescue Laura, Rossetti criticizes the Biblical Adam who, to avoid responsibility for his disobedience to God, attributes his sin to Eve. At the same time, Rossetti takes a hermeneutical approach to standard theology and re – writes the Bible from a woman's perspective, shifting the emphasis from masculine to female. Second, by focusing on Lizzie's self – sacrificial love to save Laura, Rossetti underscores Christ – likeness. Indeed, "Lizzie's call to Laura recalls Christ's words to his apostles at the last supper" (D'Amico 75):

> Come and kiss me.
> Never mind my bruises,
> Hug me, kiss me, suck my juices
> Squeezed from goblin fruits for you,
> Goblin pulp and goblin dew.
> Eat me, drink me, love me;
> Laura, make much of me:
> For your sake I have braved the glen
> And had to do with goblin merchant men.' (ll. 466-474)

The scene has frequently been subject to sexual interpretations, with connotations of lesbian homosexuality or libidinal impulse. A close survey of the context, however, reveals that the focus of the scene is not in the simple denotation of the phrases, "hug me, kiss me" and "eat me, drink me, love me," but in the character's voluntary offering of herself to redeem her depraved sister, which is rephrased as "make much of me:/For your sake I have braved the glen/And had to do with goblin merchant men." And almost miraculously, this act of self – sacrificial communion transforms the fruit juice from the beverage of intended "comfort" (l. 310) to a "fiery antidote" (l. 559) that neutralizes the "poison[ous]" fruit and restores Laura to physical and spiritual health. Rather than the sisters' homosexual relationship, this scene features a 'homo-social' love between female characters. The significance of the Eucharist scene lies in the transformation of Lizzie, from an ordinary maiden, to a Christlike figure who saves Laura by sacrificing herself.

This same scene portrays what W. Sline refers to as Rossetti's challenge to the contemporary view of women in the Nineteenth century England. According to him, it incorporates Rossetti's direct response to the conventional concept of women which was famously expressed in the male hero Romney's words in Elizabeth Barrett Browning's feminist epic, *Aurora Leigh*. A sort of a spokesman of the period, Romney states the case quite straightforwardly: women "give us doting mothers, and perfect wives,/Sublime Madonnas, and enduring saints," but they provide "no Christ," and therefore no "poet" (II. 220-225). By presenting Lizzie as a female Christ-figure, ministering the ritual of Eucharist, Rossetti tries to correct the male-dominant prejudice of Nineteenth century British society, while linking herself to E. B. Browning as the latter's immediate successor in the feminist literary tradition. The same elevation of Lizzie to the female Christ has been predicted in Florence Nightingale's work, *Cassandra*:

> "The next Christ will perhaps be a female Christ······At last there shall arise a woman, who will resume, in his own soul, all the sufferings of her race, and that woman will be the Savior of her race." (50-55).

The paradigm of Laura's change starts from her gratitude and appreciation of Lizzie's effort that was made on her behalf. Laura, otherwise self-absorbed, comes to realize that Lizzie met the goblin men "for her sake" and worries if Lizzie will become as "thirsty, canckered, and goblin – ridden" as herself. For the first time in her life, Laura tries to stand in Lizzie's position and becomes truly concerned for her, revealing the extent to which Laura has changed, i. e. from a self-indulgent, egocentric character to one who is caring, sympathetic, and genuinely appreciative of other people's love. Through suffering, she has learned the precious lesson of giving and receiving love.

> Lizzie, Lizzie, have you tasted
> For my sake the fruit forbidden?
> Must your light like mine be hidden,
> Your young life like mine be wasted,
> Undone in mine undoing
> And ruined in my ruin,
> Thirsty, cankered, goblin-ridden?' – (ll. 478-484)

The main turning point in Laura's fate takes the form of the exorcist ritual that inflicts severe pain on Laura: "Writhing as one possessed she leaped and sung/rent all her robe, and wrung/Her hands in lamentable haste,/And beat her breast" (ll. 496-9). Going through extreme suffering, Laura learns to show empathy to other people. Laura's regeneration is expressed in vivid visual description. Particularly noticeable is Rossetti's dialectical use of the fire image to describe the corrective effect of the antidotal fruit that deliberates Laura from the devastating predicament of death – in – life: the external "swift fire" merges with the existent "fire smoldering [in Laura's heart]," and finally "over[bears] its lesser flame":

Swift fire spread through her veins, knocked at her heart,
Met the fire smouldering there
And overbore its lesser flame,
She gorged on bitterness without a name:
Ah! fool, to choose such part
Of soul — consuming care!
Sense failed in the mortal strife: (ll. 507-513)

Interpreting this scene in terms of Laura's internal conflict, Bentley associates the "Swift fire" with "purifying God's law" and "the lesser flame" with "sin's law" (77). Although his allegorical reading is based on a strict dichotomy between good and evil, it seems quite persuasive considering that the image of "fire" is traditionally associated with human desire (as the fire of lust) or human spirit/soul (as the fire of purgation).

In the same vein, the merging of the two "fire[s]" assumes multiple implications of significance. First, it might indicate the meeting of two sympathetic souls: on one hand, the self-sacrifice made by Lizzie for the sake of her sister, and on the other, Laura's appreciation of sisterly love apparent in the sacrifice. Second, more immediately related to the poetic context, the dialectical merging of fires that "overbore its lesser flame" brings in a curative effect which creates Laura's sexual and psychological security. The result, Laura's restrained maturity represented in her "hug[ing] Lizzie but not twice or three times" (l. 539).

Rossetti's high valuation of Laura's care/concern for Lizzie is epitomized in the narrator's exclamatory comment on her ordeal. Here Rossetti engages the readers in the narrator's full sympathy for Laura's suffering: "Ah! fool, to choose such part./Of soul-consuming care!" Scholars have neither paid particular attention to this passage, nor have shown any effort to connect this scene to Laura's role in her own redemption. They might have taken for granted that this phrase was intended for Lizzie because she risked her life for her sister Laura.

A close look into the context, however, illuminates a possibility that this critically ignored passage is an effective device Rossetti employs to emphasize the intensity of Laura's anxiety and concern for Lizzie. In the poem, Laura's remorseful and contrite state is described in three consecutive phrases: Laura "gorged on bitterness without a name," "ch[ose] such part/Of soul – consuming care" and finally fell into a state in which "[her] Sense failed in the mortal strife." These three actions are closely and even inseparably linked together so that Laura's "mortal strife" is composed of her "gorging on bitterness" and "her soul-consuming care." In this context, it seems highly unlikely that the subject of soul-consuming care is Lizzie. Rossetti's punctuation gives a further support to such a claim. If the exclamation is articulated by Laura with Lizzie in her mind, it should be in quotes as are other sentences that express Laura's inner thoughts. This rather puzzling sentence is, however, inserted in the middle of the narrative that describes the painful curative process Laura goes through. Both in the context and in the punctuation, it seems obvious that this exclamatory phrase refers to Laura who shows her utmost gratitude and genuine concern for Lizzie.

Going through a sort of exorcist ritual, Laura restores the breached sistership into one of greater intimacy and mutual care. Laura's apparently miraculous cure is not so sudden or abrupt as has been thought: deeply rooted in mutual understanding and love, it was preconditioned by Laura's change. And since it is based on Laura's open-minded attitude toward others, Laura's regeneration does not remain on the individual level. Through the ordeal, she renews her communion with nature: that is, her suffering brings her back to the cycle of nature. Natural commemoration described in the passage elevates the entire drama of temptation – fall – redemption to a cosmic significance:

> Life out of death,
> ......
> But when the first birds chirped about their eaves,
> And early reapers plodded to the place
> Of golden sheaves,
> And dew-wet grass
> Bowed in the morning winds so brisk to pass,
> And new buds with new day
> Opened of cup-like lilies on the stream,
> Laura awoke as from a dream,
> Laughed in the innocent old way,
> Hugged Lizzie but not twice or thrice;
> Her gleaming locks showed not one thread of grey,
> Her breath was sweet as May
> And light danced in her eyes. (ll. 524-542)

Dramatic as it is moving, the rejuvenation of Laura is not a mere return to her past self: neither is it limited to Laura's initiation into adult sexuality. It is a more comprehensive kind of awakening and a step forward to maturity.

Also, because it is based on Laura's dramatic change and spiritual growth, it is sustainable and has a lasting value. Seen only from the perspective of Lizzie's unilateral sympathy and love for her sister, it is difficult to explain the scope and intensity of the change the entire poem incorporates. It is Laura's spiritual maturity that finally redeems her and endows her with the final role as the poetic voice that delivers its central theme.

Through Laura's change, Rossetti reconfirms what she has believed as a desirable operation of love which she writes about in her prose work, *The Face of the Deep*. In it she claims, "Love from without cannot accomplish its own work unless there is some response from love within" (273, qtd. D'Amico 79). Laura's cry and anxiety for her sister Lizzie is considered to be such a "sign of love from within," a precondition for Laura's self-regeneration.

4. The Role of Marginal Characters

Inseparable to the message of the redemption, the meanings/roles of Jeannie and the goblin men should be clarified. Throughout the poem Jeannie is mentioned several times by Lizzie, being related to the female heroines' surrender to temptation. As an overt victim of the promiscuous pursuit of sexual pleasure, Jeannie has a significant poetic implication. She represents a failed redemption, and an example of the negative consequences of self-indulgent desire. Without a caring sister, she meets a premature death, a symbolic device Rossetti employs to counter-balance the importance of sisterly love.

In the poem, Rossetti does not limit Jeannie's story to an individual case history. Through Lizzie's repetitious mention of the name 'Jeannie,' Rossetti produces a cumulative effect in which she features representative of the collective history/consciousness of the female community rather than a particular subject for a special case. She can be read as a symbol of women victimized in a traditional patriarchal society, an 'every woman.' It seems plausible that by replacing Jeannie with Laura, Rossetti intends to stop the tragic cycle of women's history which is composed of a series of failures and deaths, and tries to commemorate a new female hero, who should emerge from the accumulated failures of feminine effort and be able to secure her social position and independence.

In the massive drama of feminine redemption, the goblin fruit vendors assume an important role as an antagonist, giving vitality to the poem with ambivalent characteristics. With grotesque appearances, sinister behavior, and beastly energy, they appear "dangerous messengers who threaten the fabric of the security" (Campbell 8) into which people have built themselves and their family. As apparent tempters, they are feared as existing obstacles, as forbidden creatures, a submission to their temptation brings fatal damnation. Nevertheless, in the development of poetic action, the goblin men are portrayed as a necessary evil, a prerequisite for the self-development of the female heroes, Laura and Lizzie. An immediate cause of Laura's fall, they "carry keys that open the whole realm of the desired and feared adventure of the discovery of the self" (Campbell 8) of the emerging hero. Without their encounter with the goblin men, both heroines might have been "fixated on purely infantile innocence" (McGann 108). By refusing to proceed to the world of adventure, they might not have been able to achieve spiritual maturity, not to mention unable to realize the important lessons of the necessity of sharing love and the value of practicing it. In their extreme polarity, the goblin men carry out the double functions of both tempter and tester of the heroines' power and integrity. In more general terms, the goblin men stand for life's challenges necessary for the mental and spiritual development of human beings; testing human capacity to endure hardships and embrace danger in overcoming them.

In this reading focused on the change of two characters, it turned out to be Laura who experiences the more substantial change in a way that qualifies herself for regeneration. Such a reading certainly provides counter proof to many scholars' thought that the saving power of the poem comes from Lizzie's sacrificial quest for the cure of her sister. On close examination, we have found that it is no less in Laura herself than in Lizzie. In the process of poetic action, the two heroines' roles are complementary and seem evenly divided. If Lizzie initiates the redeeming process as an intercessor, it is Laura who is changed and awakened to the importance of altruistic love.

Throughout the poem, Rossetti maintains an uncensorious stance on Laura, by showing a consistently sympathetic tone, explicit in her use of metaphors and images. Lizzie's role is rather responsive and is centered around Laura. With Laura's change, the plot reaches its climax, marking a significant turning point in her destiny. Considering that Laura's change is more visible, dramatic and substantial, it seems natural that Laura acquires the speech right. Thus, in the end, now the changed Laura plays the role of rendering the ultimate message of the poem about the importance of sisterly care and love:

> 'For there is no friend like a sister
> In calm or stormy weather;
> To cheer one on the tedious way,
> To fetch one if one goes astray,
> To lift one if one totters down,
> To strengthen whilst one stands.' (ll.560-565)

In the new myth created by Rossetti, it is Laura who emerges as a new female hero. In her figuration of an emergent women's tradition, Rossetti establishes "a new female genealogy" (Maxwell 79) passing from Jeanie through Laura and Lizzie to their daughters. If Jeanie incorporates the lesson of women's failure of the past, with Laura as the turning point in women's history, the "daughters" imply that the feminist quest should be continued. As Rosenblum evaluates, "Goblin Market" represents "a rediscovery of true female origins and a rejection of the patriarchal quest myth or, rather, a reappropriation of it as a female myth" (83).

"Goblin Market" is a predominantly feminist poem, a showcase in which Christina Rossetti, a woman poet herself, explores the extent to which women put themselves in society where a male-dominant atmosphere prevails and suggests, through the communal effort of female heroes, some ways to survive in such a hostile condition and to perform significant roles in the great drama of human salvation. Represented by two female heroes, Laura and Lizzie, this massive drama covers wide-ranging issues concerning women's roles and positions, from materialized consumer items in modern capitalism to great agents of human redemption, culminating in the role of a female Christ. In this poetic narrative, Rossetti attempts to expand women's potential to the full and places women in the active core of creating a new type of community, presenting a new female myth in its creation. After all, Rossetti's vision of a hopeful future involves the building of a community where women depend on other women for support, consolation and affection. Although this new community has its own limitations because of its exclusion of male participation, this was Rossetti's answer to overcoming the crippling restrictions of the male-dominated Victorian society.

< Works Cited >

Bentley, D. M. R. "The Meretricious and the Meritorious in *Goblin Market*.: A Conjecture & an Analysis," *The Achievement of Christina Rossetti*. Ed. by David Kent. Ithaca & London: Cornell Univ. Press, 1987. pp. 57 – 81.

Brownley, M. W. "Love and Sensuality in Christina Rossetti's *Goblin Market*," *Essays in Literature*. pp.179 – 86.

Campbell, Joseph. *The Hero With a Thousand Faces*. Princeton, NJ: Princeton Univ. Press, 1968.

Casey, Janet G. "The Potential of Sisterhood: Christina Rossetti's *Goblin Market*," *Victorian Poetry*, Vol. 29, No. 1, Spring 1991. pp. 63 – 77.

Chapman, Alison. "Defining the Feminine Subject: D. G. Rossetti's Manuscript Revisions to Christina Rossetti's Poetry." *Victorian Poetry*, Vol. 35, No. 2, Summer 1997. pp. 139 – 156.

D'Amico, Diane. *Christina Rossetti: Faith, Gender, and Time*. Baton Rouge: Louisiana State Univ. Press, 1999.

Edmond, Rod. *Affairs of the Hearth: Victorian Poetry and Domestic Narrative*. London & New York: Routledge, 1988.

Gilbert, Sandra & Susan Gubar. *The Madwoman in the Attic*. New Haven & London: Yale Univ. Press, 1984.

Harrison, H. Anthony. *Victorian Poets and the Politics of Culture: Discourse & Ideology*. Charlottesville & London: Univ. Press of Virginia, 1998.

Helsinger, Elizabeth K. "Consumer Power & the Utopia of Desire: Christina Rossetti's *Goblin Market*," *Victorian Women Poets*. N. Y.: St. Martin's Press, 1995. pp. 189 – 222.

Holt, Terrence. " 'Men sell not such in any town': Exchange in *Goblin Market*." *Victorian Poetry*, Vol. 28, No. 1, Spring 1990. pp. 51 – 66.

Kent, David A. & P. G. Stanwood. *Selected Prose of Christina Rossetti*. London: Macmillan Press Ltd; 1998.

Leder, Sharon & A. Abbott. *The Language of Exclusion: The Poetry of Emily Dickinson & Christina Rossetti*. N.Y; Westport, & London: Greenwood Press, 1987.

Leighton, Angela. *Victorian Women Poets: Writing Against the Heart*. Charlottesville & London: Univ. Press of Virginia, 1992.

Maxwell, Catherine. "Tasting the Fruit Forbidden": Gender, Intertextuality, & Christian Rossetti's "Goblin Market," The Culture of Christina Rossetti. Ed. by Mary Arseneau, A. Harrison & L. J. Kooistra. Athens: Ohio Univ. Press, 1999. Pp. 75 – 104.

Mayberry, Katherine J. *Christina Rossetti & the Poetry of Discovery*. Baton Rouge & London: Louisiana State Univ. Press, 1989.

McGann, Jerome J. "Christina Rossetti's Poems," *Victorian Women Poets: A Critical Reader*. Ed. by Angela Leighton. Oxford: Blackwell Publishers, 1996.

Mermin, Dorothy. "Heroic Sisterhood in *Goblin Market*," *Victorian Poetry*, Vol. 21, 1983. pp. 107 – 118.

Morill, David F. "'Twilight is not good for maidens': Uncle Polidori & the Psychodynamics of Vampirism in *Goblin Market*." *Victorian Poetry*. Vol. 28, No. 1, Spring 1990. pp. 1 – 16.

Nightingale, Florence. *Cassandra*. Ed. by Myra Stark. Old Westbury, 1979.

Palazzo, Lynda. "The Poet & the Bible: Christina Rossetti's Feminist Hermeneutics," *The Victorian Newsletter*. Fall 1997. pp. 6 – 9.

Rosenblum, Dolores. *Christina Rossetti: The Poetry of Endurance*. Carbondale & Edwardsville: Southern illinois Univ. Press, 1986.

Rossetti, Christina. "Goblin Market," *Nineteenth –Century Women Poets*. Ed. by I. Armstrong & J. Bristow with C. Sharrock. Oxford: Clarendon Press, 1998.

pp. 524 – 36.

Sussman, Herbert. *Victorian Masculinities: Manhood and Masculine Politics in Early Victorian Literature & Art.* Cambridge Univ. Press, 1995.

III. Anxiety of Communication

Ⅲ - 1. William Wordsworth' s Anti - Linguistic Experiments With Language

Language appears as such a recurrent theme in Wordsworth's poetry that his poetic career can be defined by his multifarious experiments with language. To overcome the inherent limitations of language and to reanimate the original referentiality of words, Wordsworth turns to the essential and ultimate role of a poet, that is, the conveyance of truth. Wordsworth's primary concern is how and to what extent he can approximate his poetry to reality. His "minimal use of language" (Simpson) functions as a cardinal principle for narrowing the gap between the poetic objects and their linguistic counterparts. Based on this principle, Wordsworth invents several alternative or supplementary devices such as an emphatic notion of "real language of men," a frequent use of pre - linguistic images and an advantageous use of marginal characters.

As an ideal type of discourse, Wordsworth presents a child's non-verbal communion with nature because, he believes, in that state, one performs a perfect communication with the object even without any intervention of conventional language. His strong nostalgia for the unrecoverable notion of the ideal discourse – 'unrecoverable' because, in the Wordsworthian schema, one's experience of the perfect discourse is confined to his childhood – leads him to an almost anti-linguistic stance. As a result, he leans more and more toward silence as a more effective medium than speech for rendering the essence of life or truth.

The basis of Wordsworth's attitude toward language is an inability to believe that contemporary poetic language has the capacity to embody the eternal truth of God, nature, and the human mind. At one time, language was in God's hands, but this originally referential language has drifted further and further away from its holy beginning until empty husks are left. Within the limitations of these husks – mere shells from which the spiritual vitality has departed – man is forced to carry on his social life. Furthermore, the fossilizing influence of traditional "poetic diction" confines poetic implications to a limited scheme of conventional interpretation. Now, "poetic diction" becomes a "counter-spirit" ("Essays on Epitaph," No. 2, 65) with its tyrannizing power, while stifling the potential referentiality of poetic language.

This tragic awareness of the artificiality, the emptiness, the conventionality of language preconditions Wordsworth's notion of the "real language of man," or "language really used by men." Wordsworth's "real language of man" was at first a main mechanism through which he could come to terms with the stereotypical connotations of traditional "poetic diction." By reanimating the "living voice" (Prelude, VI, 111) and the original referentiality of the words, he thought he could provide a new vehicle which was able to "carry meaning to the natural heart;/To tell us what is passion, what is truth,/What reason, what simplicity and sense" (*Prelude* VI, 111 – 14). Just as he was not comfortable with the excessive artificiality of the eighteenth – century poetic diction, so was he not complacent regarding the limits of human communication which, to a certain extent, was an inherent defect of language itself.

The double challenge – one, from the traditional poetic diction and the other, from the inherent limitations of language – which Wordsworth undertakes is manifested in his first collection of poems, *Lyrical Ballads*. Several poems from this collection not only display different aspects of linguistic experiments, but also question the capacity of language which functions as an instrument of reality. In fact, Wordsworth's concern with language goes far beyond the declared purpose of the volume – that is, his intention to test "how far the language of conversation in the middle and lower classes of society is adapted to the purposes of poetic pleasure." It is more profound and comprehensive than a mere test of the availability and validity of rustic language in poetry – more profound in that he probes into the duality of nature of language operating both as an agent of socialization and of symbolic deprivation of the self, and more comprehensive in that he observes language in terms of its organic relationships with people, living circumstance, and lifestyle.

For Wordsworth, language, as a necessary tool for one's socialization, is not a separate phenomenon of communicative activity: it is an integral part of the human mind. The performative function of language is heavily dependent on its user and the place in which it is spoken. In his "Preface" to *Lyrical Ballads*, Wordsworth declares freshness and simplicity to be the primary yardstick of the "real language of man." Likewise, he theorizes that linguistic durability and purity are acquired by the humility of living close to nature and the consequent artless and unaffected lifestyle. Compared to the dead and worn-out linguistic signs and meaningless labels on the walls of London (as described in the *Prelude*, VII), rustic language is acknowledged as the more "permanent and philosophical" in conveying the truth. In its purity and rejuvenating force, Wordsworth's "language of nature" is equivalent to the "original Logos, the act of immediate calling into being whereby God had literally 'spoken the world' " (Christ 41).

The poem, "The Last of the Flock" is an introductory poem insofar as Wordsworth's reactionary attitude toward conventional norm of manners is concerned. David Sampson – in his 1984 article entitled "Wordsworth and the Deficiencies of Language" – interprets Wordsworth's reaction against conventional manners in terms of his anti-"poetic diction" stance. According to him, in Wordsworth's poetry, rural speech functions "not as an actual model but as a symbolic goal, representative of a style as liberated from conventional rules as the farmer's grief" (61). He rightly points out that in this poem, what matters is "the narrator's inability to comprehend not why the man is weeping but why *a healthy adult is weeping publicly*" (emphases added, 61). In fact, the farmer is inevitably controlled by traditional norm: he feels "shame" for his public display of emotion and "turn[s] aside,/As if he wish (es) himself to hide" (ll. 11-12).

Wordsworth's display of the farmer's desperate situation in which he has to choose between his children and his flock attests to Wordsworth's critical stand on society. Through his compassionate portrayal of the farmer as a central figure, Wordsworth, on the one hand, reinforces the significance of the humble people and the value of their altruistic love for non-human creatures; on the other hand, he indirectly expresses his critical opinion of the contemporary socio-economic system which cannot guarantee even the farmer's humble living. Wordsworth's defense of the farmer's situation is just another version of his justification of rustic language as a proper poetic language. Certainly, Wordsworth uses this anecdote as a dramatic protest against "the stylistic rule" (Sampson 61) and the established value system which have forbidden any deviations or variations from conventional mode.

In another poem, "The Thorn," Wordsworth's approach to language is more substantial and specific than that in "The Last of the Flock." By tracing a mythopoeic transformation of an ordinary event, Wordsworth challenges the validity of a story or a legend which uses language as a main tool. Language here becomes the overriding concern of the poem. It is not merely the subject of the poem, but the whole action of the poem is involved with the problem of language – of how a story generates, how much reality can be embodied in human language, and to what extent it can be shared between human beings.

The narrative frame of the poem is constructed on the principle of repetition and tautology. The narrator, an old sea-captain, recurrently returns to similar passages, places, and descriptions, and he even repeats the tediously insinuating tone; likewise, the woman character Martha Ray repeatedly ejaculates her laments in a double version of "Oh misery! Oh misery!" and "Oh woe is me! Oh misery!." While centripetally highlighting the poetic center – that is, an old thorn, a nearby muddy pond, a woman in red cloak, and a heap, "like an infant's grave in size" (l. 52) – this technique of repetition and tautology contributes to creating an atmosphere of incantational superstition.

Wordsworth, in his note for this poem, makes it clear that the use of tautology is a dramatization of "the inadequateness of our powers" and of the "deficiencies of language" (140). This claim is further supported by Frances Ferguson who observes – in her excellent study of Wordsworth's poetry entitled *Language as Counter-Spirit* – that tautology in the poems of Lyrical Ballads including this poem is "less as poverty than as an intensity" (18) of poetic effect. Also, in this context, the narrator is interpreted "less as a character than as a characteristic way of talking; he is almost an embodiment of the figure of repetition" (Ferguson 13).

Consequently, the unreliability and the gossipy quality of the story of Martha Ray and her alleged infanticide evoke several speculations on Wordsworth's attitude toward language and human perception. Most conspicuously, Wordsworth alludes to the potential vulnerability of all human beings to misjudgment and misunderstanding, especially when we depend only on a linguistic medium. By using an exquisite technique, he gradually engages the reader in the same process of making up stories and legends, even without the reader's recognition. His openly inviting gesture – such as "I wish that *you would go*" (l. 109). "sad cases, *as you may think*" (l.

146), and "*You must take care and chuse your time* /The mountain when to cross" (emphases added. ll. 58 – 59) – has even a mesmeric effect for prompting the (perhaps, even reluctant) reader's involvement into the poetic action. This rhetorical strategy itself seems to be a metaphorical illustration of Wordsworth's intention that he does not exclude the possibility of the reader's fallibility in case when reality is clarified otherwise.

The same technique further stresses Wordsworth's critical attitude toward established claims that truth and reality can be known and shared. He points out the fictitiousness of a story or a legend. In fact, the whole event in the poem is exhibited merely as an accumulation of gossips and groundless beliefs which are conceived through several layers of consciousness – the village people's, the narrator's, the poet's and even the reader's. Nevertheless, several things remain obscure until the end of the narration: Did Martha Ray really killed her baby? Was it the baby's face that the narrator saw in the pond? Or, was Martha Ray really mad?

Wordsworth's avoidance of locating any authentic source of the story reveals his main attitude toward language and perception. He illustrates how difficult it is to figure out the truth, how puzzling and unstable a linguistic medium appears for rendering the truth, and therefore, how unreasonable and absurd it might be to unconditionally accept certain established notion of language, story and poetry.

Wordsworth's extreme sensitivity to the insufficiency of language in incarnating the real feature of the poetic ideas brings forth his sceptical response to the children's initiation into the linguistic community. For, in his system, as is schematized in his "Ode, Intimations of Immortality," a child lives closest to the ideal state in his perfect communion with nature in which he does not require, and even repudiates, the intervention of linguistic medium. Two poems from *Lyrical Ballads* are collared by such a skeptical overtone about the meddling intellect of the adult by means of language. In "Anecdote for Fathers," and "We Are Seven," the very exchange of conversation between characters attests to the inefficiency of language as a communicative mode.

In both poems, children's participation in the adult's verbal community is depicted as involuntary, forced, and thus, negative. In "Anecdote for Fathers," the boy Edward's linguistic spontaneity – and further, his free will, is frustrated by his father's urge for an immediate response to "matters (both) uninteresting to (him), (and to) which (he) had no decided opinion" (Wordsworth 134). Meanwhile, in "We Are Seven," the little maid's vision of the world and life is disturbed by the adult's imposition of the way to see and express things within a certain norm. For the eight-year-old girl, the narrator's enforcement of the fixed notion of death – death, as an eternal nullification/annihilation of one's existence on earth – and of the numerical view of the human relationship is only irritating; for the boy, the father's double abuse through his rhetorical tactics – first, by his almost mesmeric manipulation of the boy's psychology, and then, by his repeated urge to reason such a psychology – can only double his lie. In these poems, children are charged with multiple burdens that are projected from outside by the adults: the girl, with the unacceptable notion of death, "the inability of language to express (her) vision of death" (Christie 44), and the insensitive adult's multi-dimensionally numerical world view; the boy, by the forced choice and the subsequent demand for rationalizing that choice.

In consequence, both the little maid and the boy are presented as victims of "linguistic and peculiarly human distortion forced by the myopic adult consciousness" (Christie 44). If we consider that the boy's relationship to the narrator in "Anecdote for Fathers" is the closest imaginable one between son and father, the victimization of the boy appears more perverted and more vulnerable than the girl's case. In fact, in "We Are Seven," the girl's obstinate adherence to her own opinion – that is, still they are seven, in spite of the death of the two siblings – functions as a weapon to protect her from a loss and further victimization of the self. Meanwhile, at the end of "Anecdote for Fathers," even the narrator's ambiguous comment on the "lore" he learned from his son is nothing more than an evasive gesture of appeasing his guilty conscience. Even though the narrator was, from the start, aware of what he was doing and though he pushed his son into such a baffling situation merely "in very idleness" (l. 20), his action is not justified: it is still insensitive and selfish, and the result is injurious – perhaps, even traumatic for the innocent boy. In these two poems, Wordsworth illustrates the failure of communication and understanding between human beings: he questions not only the possibility of true communication between human beings but also, to a certain extent, the effectiveness of the children's exposure to linguistic community at all.

The limited fixation of the child's linguistic vision is once more demonstrated through irony in the poem "Alice Fell," – through the gap between the real issue of the poem and the narrator's understanding of the situation. Although Alice's pre-verbal outcry succeeds in evoking the narrator's charitable mind, the ensuing conversation between the gentleman and the girl shows a great lack of understanding. The narrator who is accustomed to seeing reality as only expressed in language cannot figure out the deeper cause of the girl's sorrow than the entangled cloak in the wheel, that is, her orphanage and her "belong (ing) to Durham." In his limited vision, he considers that his charitable act of purchasing a new cloak for the girl would guarantee her utmost happiness. Even the narrator's self-satisfied comment on the girl's pride on a new cloak is no less than a reflection of his own blind self-exaltation. For the time being, the simple child may be deceived by the very simplicity of her mind and trapped by her inability of fully expressing herself in the exact terms that the adult demands. Despite a temporary relief of the tragic situation through the narrator's charitable act, the main concern of the poem remains unresolved.

Ironically enough, the failure of language in clarifying human relationship and associating man to man with mutual understanding seems to be the primary motivating factor for Wordsworth to preach more and more "one brotherhood of all the human race" (Prelude, XII, 88), "the universal heart" (Prelude XII, 219), and "the very heart of man" (Prelude XIII, 240). Perhaps, Wordsworth may well have convinced that the deepest truth cannot and should not depend on the transient and arbitrary medium of words.

As a result, the more he confronts the limits of language, the more he tries to retreat into an anti-linguistic stance ('anti-linguistic,' in the sense of its being not systematized by linguistic rules) in which one cannot but accept the naked essence of reality. His device of "language really used by man" is better understood in this context, for as far as human society is concerned, this language is supposed to be the closest to the essence of reality because of its rejection of linguistic ornament and excessive artificiality.

Wordsworth's frequent use of pre-linguistic utterances (such as crying, moaning, shouting, laughter, weeping, etc) as well as marginal characters (such as the mad mother, the idiot boy, etc) is thus a result of his effort to preserve the genuine feelings of men, to secure the most immediate appeal to the reader, to approximate his poetry to reality, and to make up for the deficiencies of language. These devices draw the reader's special attention not only because they are almost unprecedented, but also because those sounds and abnormal characters occupy the poetic center in certain poems. Wordsworth certainly shows, through such a valiant attempt, that the common truth can be conveyed and shared prior to any linguistic-sifting or selective reasoning process.

If we consider that pre-linguistic utterances appear dominant in the poems about children and objects of nature, Wordsworth must have presumed that such auditory images can be used as a powerful medium through which he can bring human discourse closer to the ideal state. In the poems "Alice Fell" and "The Idle Shepherd-Boys," the poor girl Alice's crying and the sheep's moaning take the center of the poetic action. As is discussed above, in "Alice Fell," the girl's cry calls for an immediate response of the passer-by gentleman and becomes a guide for his proper acts of charity. Likewise, the whole action of "The Idle Shepherd-Boys" is evolved from the moaning of an endangered sheep. At the "piteous moan"

(l. 60) of the lamb that "had slipped into the stream" (l. 67), the shepherd's heart "dies," his "pulse stopped, his breath is lost, (and)/He totters, pallid as a ghost" (ll. 62 – 63). The shepherd's idle joy in nature suddenly yields to a sense of guilt for his neglect of duty and the pastoral scene is changed into almost a seat of judgment by the passer-by poet's upbraiding of the shepherd's idleness.

In addition to their appeal to the most elemental feelings of the reader, by virtue of the intensity of the communication they generate, the pre-linguistic articulations turn out to be a better medium than sophisticated linguistic expressions. Indeed, such efficacy of the pre-verbal sounds even replaces the inspirational function of the conventional 'muse': the immediate and primordial articulations become an incentive for the poet's creation of poems.

Wordsworth's transformation of marginal characters into central poetic figures is a continuation of his effort to preserve and communicate the purity of human mind as well as linguistic spontaneity. Wordsworth's use of marginal characters, of course, entails a danger of double contradiction because it may result in a total communication block. Or, perhaps, the ordinary person who is engaged in a discourse with the abnormal characters may interpret the whole situation in his own way. In the poems, however, Wordsworth's compassionate attitude towards the abnormal characters which is achieved through his 'wise – passiveness' – his ability to fully empathize with his characters – renounces any possibility of the normal man's one – sided imposition of unfair oppression of them. Wordsworth portrays the marginal characters as the pathetic hero (ine) of his poems.

Since the characters are abnormal, and impaired, either mentally or linguistically (in the sense of the socialized language), nobody can victimize them with his imposition of linguistic norms or with preconceived notions of the objects. The fact that the mad-mother and the idiot boy show their emotions in the most natural and uninhibited way proves that they are free from social impositions of language. The preservation of unsophisticated and uncontaminated linguistic ability is, to a certain extent, due to their mental abnormality or retardation: that is, in Wordsworth's poems, the marginal characters' mental deficiency is recompensed by their linguistic and emotional purity.

In "Mad-Mother," the female character's unremitting overflow of love for her baby is juxtaposed with another emotional conflict between her love and hate for her husband who deserted her. Through the woman's one-sided discourse with the infant boy, Wordsworth demonstrates that an ideal discourse rests less on the conversation than on the speaker's underlying emotion. In fact, the boy's sucking itself replaces language, and more than that. It becomes a more powerful response to the woman's speaking than any eloquent speech that is imaginable. The woman's discourse with the baby secures a self-contained happiness as long as the baby sucks her breast.

Nevertheless, as soon as the body contact between the sucking mother and her baby is severed, the woman's happy vision suddenly changes into horror and hatred. She sees "wicked looks" instead of "the sweetest" face of the baby: "Where are thou gone my own dear child?/What wicked looks are those I see?" (ll. 85-86). She experiences a kind of anti-epiphanic moment in which her hate and fear for her husband momentarily outweighs her love for the baby, only to be replaced by her expectation of a happy life with the baby. This free-flowing orchestration of complex human feelings might hardly be achieved by any common custom-bound people. Wordsworth's almost pathological accuracy as to the mad woman's internal state of mind is achieved by modern writers only through skillful inventions such as stream – of – consciousness and dramatic – or interior – monologue.

Likewise, "The Idiot Boy" dramatizes the idiot – boy Johnny's spontaneous joy found in nature, but the boy's relationship with his mother, Betty, raises another clash between child and adult in terms of language and perception. Although Betty's devotional love for her son allows her joy at the boy's "burr – " sounds, she cannot quite understand her son's linguistic spontaneity, not to mention his perfect harmony with nature. For her, nature is still replete with hidden elements of danger and fear. Her fretfully detailed "what to follow, what to shun./What to do, and what to leave undone,/How turn to left, and how to right" (ll. 64-66) is joyously repudiated by the boy, in part, by his inability to understand Betty's instruction and, in part, by his exuberant joy in tranquil nature.

Insofar as Wordsworth's search for an ideal type of discourse is concerned, "The Idiot Boy" provides a successful test case. In this poem, Wordsworth succeeds in a complete repudiation of the adult's intellectual and linguistic meddling and secures the child's perfect communion with nature at the same time. Wordsworth's juxtaposition, line by line, of "the owlets hoot and the owlets curr" (l. 114) and Johnny's "burr, burr, burr" (l. 115), on the one hand, seems to reinforce the boy's perfect union with nature. On the other hand, the boy's extremely satisfactory journey through the forests becomes a witness of the failure of language in integrating human experience. "All (the boy's) travel" of joy and spontaneity, when expressed in language, degenerates into two seemingly incomprehensible sentences: "The cocks did crow to-whoo, to-whoo,/And the sun did shine so cold" (ll. 460-461). These same sentences, however, from the vantage point of the boy, are the very incarnation of the boy's unity with nature: in his utmost joy, the darkness of night is transformed into a harmony of music and light. Even the joyous tone of the poem, being in line with the idiot boy's congenial state of mind, seems to mock at the so-called normal mind and its notions of the communication.

The boy's ecstatic experience with nature is intensified in a short poem, "There Was A Boy," which later was included in *The Prelude*, Book V. In this poem, Wordsworth's aspiration for exploring an ideal discourse reaches its climax. He achieves that goal by scheming the process of the boy's communion with nature, from his mimetic imitation, to his silent discourse with nature, and through his absent discourse with the narrator after his death.

The ideal discourse Wordsworth embodies in this poem is represented in his exclusion of conversations between human beings. Neither the boy nor the narrator is involved with another person: the boy tries a discourse with the owl, and then with nature in silence, and the narrator with the dead boy by his grave side. The boy's primary language is mimetic: he imitates the owl's hooting and waits for its response. Meanwhile, the narrator's is meditative and self-generative because his discourse with the dead boy is carried out in contemplative silence.

More emphatic than Wordsworth's exclusion of human speech from the ideal discourse is his special inclination for the moment of silence. In Wordsworth's perception of the interaction between language and silence, silence itself is recognized as a type of discourse in which truth 'speaks' more powerfully than linguistic utterance. For instance, as A. W. Phinney mentions it as "the acme of the Romantic dream" (67), the revelation of truth is not even located in the boy's mimetic correspondence with the owl, but in the moment of silence:

> And, when there came a pause
> Of silence such as baffles his best skill:
> Then, sometimes, in that silence, while he hung
> Listening, a gentle shock of mild surprise
> Has carried far into his heart the voice
> Of mountain − torrents; or the visible scene
> Would enter unawares into his mind
> With all its solemn imagery, its rocks,
> Its woods, and that uncertain heaven received
> Into the bosom of the steady lake. (ll. 16-25).

Only when his "best self" is "baffled" and he is "hung listening," can the boy catch the "voice" of nature and see the beauty of natural scenery.

The boy's early death in the poem, nevertheless, suggests that Wordsworth's yearning for ideal discourse is an unrealizable dream. As one cannot reject his growth, so is it impossible for one to do without language so long as he lives in society. For Wordsworth this dilemma is recognized as a condition of the human being. Perhaps, the prevailing elegiac mood of his poems may partly explain his sad awareness of the existential condition of human life. If we consider that in Wordsworth's poems children meet an early death almost without exception, this claim is further justified. Wordsworth's ideal of the perfect communication fades away into eternal silence with the passing away of the boy – and by inference, the poet's own boyhood – and he cherishes the memory of past experience through a silent intercourse with the dead boy by the grave side.

The poet's silent "half an hour" discourse by the grave side is, undoubtedly, self-generative, reflexive, and circular because it is carried out in his own mind. It is shaped around "emotion recollected in tranquility," the very foundation of the poetry that Wordsworth qualifies in his "Preface to *Lyrical Ballads*." At this point, Wordsworth's notion of the ideal discourse and his definition of poetry are finally integrated in the form of the grave-side meditation, the epitaph. As Susan E. Meisenhelder points out, for Wordsworth, epitaph is "the paradigmatic poem" (24) and the act of poetic creation is identified with the process of silent discourse with the past through memory. Any poetic creation is after all the poet's regenerating effort of the past by retrieving it through meditative reflection. For just as one cannot transcend his mortality, so a linear human experience cannot be redeemed. Wordsworth's special interest in the epitaphic mode thus can be regarded as his conscious effort to reconcile the eternal conflict between mutability of humans and his yearning for immortality, between his desire for sharing by expressing himself and that for preservation by keeping silent, and even between his backward glance to the past and his vision for the future.

Wordsworth's notion of the ideal discourse is retrogressive, exclusive, circular, and thus, destined to end in failure. It resounds only in the elegiac mood of the poems. But his experiments with language are not so much disappointing as his unrealizable dream of perfect communication. The challenge which Wordsworth had to undertake turns out to be a sound motivation for him to prepare a new poetic era in which the poet's consciousness of language becomes a central issue of poetic creation. Likewise, his invention of several complementary devices and rhetorical strategies have helped to expand the scope of communication and to widen the substantial realm of language in poetry.

Perhaps, from the first, he may have been well aware of the limitations of his experiments with poetic language. For "the utmost we can know, (through language)/Both of ourselves and of the universe" (*Prelude*, VII, 645-46) is "the label" of the "Blind Beggar — wearing a written paper, to explain/His story, whence he came, and who he was" (*Prelude*,VII, 639-42). Nevertheless, through his experiments, Wordsworth comes to terms with the "sad incompetence of human speech" and further with the reality reflected in it. Above all, his reaffirmation of the fact that man once had experienced perfect communication with nature becomes a sustaining power for the poet's continuous pursuit of his profession as a craftsman of words. From the reservoir of the past which is preserved in the memory (metaphorically in the tomb of the dead boy), the poet continuously draws out power for coping with reality. Like the actor (*Prelude*, VII) who has to play the role of 'absence' with a written prop with the word "invisible" on his back, Wordsworth still has to write his poetry in language believing that silence often makes a better medium of communication.

< Works Cited >

Bostetter, Edward E. *The Romantic Ventriloquists: Wordsworth, Coleridge, Keats, Shelley, Byron.* Seattle & London: Univ. of Washington Press, 1975.

Christi, Will. "Wordsworth and the Language of Nature." *Wordsworth Circle,* 14 (1), Winter, 1983: 40 – 46.

Ferguson, Frances. *Language as Counter-Spirit.* New Haven & London: Yale Univ. Press, 1977.

Grosart, Alexander B. Edited. *The Prose Works of William Wordsworth,* Vol. 2. New York: AMS Press, 1967.

Hutchinson, Thomas. Edited. *Wordsworth: Poetical Works.* Oxford & New York: Oxford Univ. Press, 1985.

Maxwell, J. C. *William Wordsworth: The Prelude, A Parallel Text.* New York: Penguin Books Ltd; 1971.

Meisenhelder, Susan E. *Wordsworth's Informed Reader: Structures of Experience in His Poetry.* Nashville, Tennessee: Vanderbilt Univ. Press, 1988.

Owen, A, J. Edited. *Wordsworth and Coleridge: Lyrical Ballads 1798.* Oxford: Oxford Univ. Press, 1969.

Phinney, A. W. "Wordsworth's Winander Boy and Romantic Theories of Language." *Wordsworth Circle,* 18 (1), Winter, 1987: 66 – 72.

Sampson, David. "Wordsworth and 'The Deficiencies of Language'." *ELH* 51 (1), 1984: 53 – 68.

Simpson, David. *Irony and Authority in Romantic Poetry.* Totowa, New Jersey: Rowman and Littlefield, 1979.

III - 2. Seamus Heaney's Exploration of Language in "Glanmore Sonnets": A Poetic Imperative

Seamus Heaney's writing has been an effort to balancing the intimate but intricately subtle relationship between the act of literary production and specific political involvement - an effort, in his own terms, to satisfying "the poet's dual responsibility to tell a truth as well as to make things" (qtd. Williams 324). Such an effort has recurrently appeared in his early poems, but it is the most self-conscious and explicit in his 1979 collection of poems, *Field Work*. His sonnet sequence in this volume, eutitled "Glanmore Sonnets," deserves a special attention. As an art poem dealing with the business of writing, this sequence makes a turning point in Heaney's attitude toward his profession as a poet and his role as a *Northern Irish poet* (emphases added). In this work, Heaney aims at locating his poetic goal and succeeds in achieving it by means of an in - depth exploration of the nature and function of language.

As in most meta-poems, this sequence shows the poet's heavy dependence on language: its theme is the significance of the exploration of language; its subject matter is the poet's experience with language on both personal and tribal level. Ironically, such an attitude is an outgrowth of Heaney's treasuring of silence in his earlier poems published before this work. It has more to do with his religious and community background than with his individual personality. Born, grown, and educated in a Catholic tradition in rural Irish country, Heaney shares with his family and neighbors the idea of putting silence over speech as a sort of tribal virtue. "Whatever you say, say nothing" (qtd. Morrison 23) was a piece of wisdom Heaney heard from his mother.

The common quality of Heaney's earlier characters is their lack of speech and according to Morrison, Heaney himself takes the position of "valuing silence over speech, of defending the shy and awkward against the confident and the accomplished, of feeling language to be a kind of betrayal" (23). If he remains reticent in his earlier poems, especially, as for the immediate social issue, that is, the religious conflict between the Protestants and the Catholics in Belfast, in "Glanmore Sonnets," Heaney exerts a conscious effort to convert the previous tribal silence into poetic speech by finding out some connection between speech and silence, by drawing out speech from the "deep no sound" of Irish legacy embedded in his subconsciousness. Metaphorically, through this sequence, Heaney is digging out a "bog" of his earlier poems to retrieve the buried treasure, some unique Irish experience and tribal wisdom. For him, his Irishness, crystalized in the tribal silence, provides a *raison d'etre* for his poetic articulation and endows his poem with life and power. It becomes his poetic inspiration.

In his poetic manifesto, Heaney's speculation of language is widely varied. His concern with language encompasses his thoughts about the mystery of the origin and workings of sounds and images, the etymological uncovering of words, and the examination of the triangular relationship among language, tradition, and poetry. In his treatment of language, Heaney is exceptionally specific and precise. He even avoids using the general term "language"; instead he subdivides language into several related and compositional notions such as vowels, sounds, verses and images. After all, language is neither a simple poetic medium nor an abstract notion for him. Communicating multifarious layers of meanings, the scope of language is extended to the core of the poetic sensibility of a whole race. As an organic force, language, then, unites, as T. S. Eliot has said, "the most ancient and the most civilized mentality." In this poem, Heaney delves into the "subsoil" of language to find out "what's lost, [but which] is never lost forever" (Kinahan 413), and in this process, his exploration of language parallels his poetic creation.

Except for Sonnets VIII, IX, and X — in which Heaney seems to be more concerned with human relationships than the problem of language — the other seven sonnets are closely interwoven not only in structure, but also in images and poetic ideas. While remaining self-contained by virtue of its strict 14-line formality and rhyming pattern, each sonnet "reassures the presence of the other sonnets" (Bedient 118) by consistently turning to similar images and their implications. Also, though slow, the whole sequence shows a thematic development moving into Heaney's assertion of the poet's role and his reaffirmation of the excavation of language as a poetic necessity.

For his poetic subject, Heaney employs his personal experience, specifically, his childhood and his recent recluse to the "strange loneliness" (III, L. 10) at Glanmore Castle. Not only his pastoral life is completely sketched into the poem, it also becomes an effective means of elucidating the rather abstract poetics. Even though the language and imagery used in the sequence are mixture of the concrete and the abstract, the specific and the general, and the literal and the metaphorical, the familiarity and concreteness of the poetic material promote the reader's understanding. Thus, the subtle intellectual complexity of the poetic idea is conveyed in an unusually accessible way.

Heaney's thesis, the poet as a ploughman of words, is clarified in the opening sonnet: "Vowels ploughed into other: opened ground" (l. 11). That he mentions 'vowels' rather than 'consonants' as the primary element of poetry indicates that his notion of poetry is basically emotional and feminine. It is also noticeable that Heaney's sudden juxtaposition of the "two separate ideas of farming and farming words, sense, and feelings" (Bedient 119), in addition to his flexible application of abundant agrarian images, is not a mere metaphysical conceit, but a clear indication of his unusual degree of originality and creativity. Intensified by the concrete verbal images implied in words such as "breathe," "open," "steam," "quickèn," and finally, "Easter," the poet's "enactment of rural toil" (Curtis 117) is presented affirmative and fertile so much so that it is finally elevated to the ritual of rebirth and resurrection.

Heaney's use of metaphor is extensive, meticulous, and accurate. Round the controlling metaphor of the farmer-poet's agrarian engagement, each stage of literary activity makes a one-to-one correspondence to that of the field work. As an initiator and witness of the fecundity of the earth, the poet anticipates a "good life" (I, l. 6), a wish for a good harvest doubly meaningful for both the farmer and the poet. Immediately following is a new definition of art – "art a paradigm of earth new from the lathe/Of plough" (I, ll. 7-8). The metaphorical expression of the poetic wish, however, soon assumes a symbolic significance when it reaches "the fundamental dark unblown rose" (I, l. 11), presumably, some of the uniquely mysterious, essential and rich cultural assets of Ireland.

The clarified poetic aim governs the way how the poet develops his ideas of poetry and poetics. Heaney makes each sonnet organic and contributory to his poetry — making which concurrently takes place with his presentation of poetics. Once established his poetic goal, the poet anticipates the "organic activity of imagination" (Bedient 119). For Heaney, the search for imagination, however, goes backward rather than forward. Instead of envisioning future, it withdraws into his childhood memory, the bygone past, and his deep subconsciousness. He does not actively search for it, either. He "wait[s] then ,···" (I, l. 12) passively, anxiously, and probably, with great endurance and tension, as if he knows "what it is to have to wait before the writing can begin" (Williams 324). Then, in an unexpected way, the poet experiences a rush of imaginative energy from which his "ghosts" appear in "sowers aprons," and spread "the dream grain" on the poetic field.

The unpredictability of the activity of imagination is further emphasized in the second sonnet where Heaney juxtaposes the mystery of the origin and the spontaneous cooperation of the words with thought. In order to convey the idea that words emerge mysteriously from the dark and deep subconscious, Heaney employs images of moving creatures: "*Sensings, mountings* from the hiding places.···. *entering*··· *ferreting* themselves out of their dark hutch"(emphases added, II, ll. 1-3). For him, language is alive and procreative: the overflowing words approach the "sense of touch," "sensing," "mounting," "entering," and "ferreting themselves." Once they have come, the words dictate and demand the matching poetic rhythm, image and even the corresponding thought, just as the image of the stone is a response to the sculptor's tool.

In a more perceptive way Heaney focuses, in Sonnet IV, on the mysteriousness with which a poet catches sounds and images. The poet's childhood experience of catching sounds along the railroad "with an ear to the line" (IV. l. 1) provides a fit illustration of how unexplainable, accidental and intuitive one's capturing of words, sounds, and images is. As words emerge in a mysterious way, so do images and sounds rise spontaneously and vanish unknowingly into "where they seemed to start" (IV, l. 14). In this context, the whole cycle of emerging, operating, and vanishing of sounds, images and words is defined in a single term, "mystery."

The supposition that language is alive to the poet may sound cliche to most of us, but it is not so with Heaney. He believes that the liveliness of language itself is the main dynamics through which a poet can have access to, and retrieve the tradition and historical past of his race. In Sonnet II, he hopes to "raise a voice [which] might continue, hold, dispel, [and] appease" (II, ll. 11 – 12) "from the backs of ditches of the hedge-school of Glanmore." He wishes to touch "some inner, intimate keynote" (Kinahan 414) through which he would stand side by side with traditional Irish bards who had recited songs and stories to the "slug-horn" and the "slow-chanter." Here Heaney aspires to seek poetic inspiration from Ireland's past that goes as far back as the Celtic Twilight.

Throughout the whole sequence, and particularly in Sonnets II and IV, Heaney takes the Romantic poets' notion of poetry. For Heaney, since the linguistic elements of poetry, i. e. words, sounds, and images rise mysteriously and work spontaneously, a poem rises by itself, too – a perfect reminder of Wordsworth's definition of the Romantic poem: a "spontaneous overflow of powerful feelings." Likewise, Heaney's notion of the poet is basically Romantic and he continuously puts himself in the position of a poet who "waits" and takes rather than the one who makes and seeks. Heaney seems to suggest that, as long as a poets turns to language for resource of his poetry, he is a "passive receptacle" in Eliot's terms, or a "taker" (Samuels 34) instead of an originator.

As a carrier of sensory experience of man, language helps to shape human perception. In Sonnet III, Heaney traces the sequential development of human perception from sound (He heard the songs of "the cuckoo and the corncrake"), to sight (He "saw" that "a baby rabbit/Took his bearings" out on the field), and to the cognitive workings of mind (He "knew" that "the deer/Were careful under larch and May-green spruce"). Whether remaining in a pre-utterance stage or not, language conveys sensory experiences to man and helps him to understand the mode of the existence of other creatures. Particularly in this sonnet, Heaney shows an exquisite craftsmanship as he transforms the raw material of his rich sensory experience in nature into a valid poetic form by manipulating rhythms and sounds.

Since Heaney's notion of poetry is basically Romantic, his "comparing [his wife and himself] to two [William and Dorothy Wordsworth]" is not a thing to surprise. With relation to this, one can notice that, in spite of his declared search for Irish legacy, Heaney does not seem to consider Yeats as his immediate poetic model: instead, he implies Wordsworth to be his model. His adherence to the iambic, the most dominant rhythm of English poetry, his Wordsworthian empathy with nature, and his sympathetic response to natural surroundings, all characterize his attitude toward the main stream of English literature and Romanticism. In a more specific way, Heaney prepares a channel for himself to join the great masters of English poetry. Above all, his intimate response to nature leads him to the camp of Romantic nature poets. He draws rhythms and cadences (e. g. birdsong) from natural surroundings: the evening was "all crepuscular and iambic" (III, l. 3); the breeze outside is "cadences" (III, l. 14). Second, his complacent life with his wife in a pastoral county, Wicklow, offers a solid ground of connecting him to Wordsworth. He enjoys rather idyllic life without concern of terrible religious turbulence in Belfast, just as "Dorothy and William" (III, l. 11) did at Dove Cottage. In spite of his wife's tone of surprise and hesitation, Heaney's mention of Dorothy and Wordsworth as their counterpart is an irresistible indication that he is sensitive to the place he takes in English literature and wants to include himself in the main stream.

As language unites people of different places and times, as an embodiment of human experience, it widens the scope and realm of human existence. Heaney probes into such power of language on a personal level (Sonnet V) and on an ethnic level (Sonnet VI). In the poet's etymological analysis of the variations of words ("bower tree" – "boortree" – "elderberry"), language, as an ontological entity, assumes various perspectives and implications according to the growth of the mind. By exemplifying his childhood experience of learning names of things and of playing "touching tongues" game, Heaney demonstrates how "feelings [can be] activated by the sounds of syllables" (Perkins 481). He is unusually responsive to the ring of the words, their "texture," their connotation, and their ultimate power. For him, language is a principal agent for integrating human experience. Reminding one of the Wordsworth's notion of "spots of time," Heaney shows how words, which have originated intuitively from a sensory experience in childhood ("touching tongues" games), become an incentive to an adult's rich and vivid re-experience of the past.

Only through the role of an etymologist, can a poet recapture the fetal experience of his past which lies buried deep in his subconscious level. The poet's sensory experience of the past, in turn, enriches his poetic language with ample connotations. Such mutual indebtedness between language and experience underlies his wish for return to the image of womb: "I fall back to my tree-house and would crouch/Where small buds shoot and flourish in the hush." Heaney's selection of an archetypal childhood game, "touching tongues" ("tongue" as the very place of articulation in which a sound is shaped) and the mixture of verb tenses including an incomplete verb form, "would," (in "would crouch") is quite intentional: he demonstrates the extent to which he relies on language in his poetic creation. Through his self-assigned role as the "etymologist of roots and graftings" (V, l. 12), Heaney reinforces the cyclical function of language in the communication of human experience. In fact, the following comment by Heaney on a Russian poet Mandelstam might be properly applied to this explication:

> Mandelstam had an etymological imagination, a belief that language is not only the sea upon which the ship of the poem sails, but the element from which the ship is fashioned –

something, I suppose, like a water bubble sailing on water.
(qtd. Kinahan 413).

In Sonnet VI, the scope and efficacy of the experience with language is generalized and extended to a tribal dimension: now, this experience goes beyond personal memory and becomes a legend, a myth. As an elaboration of the last sestet of Sonnet II, a "story" here is a "rejuvenat[ing]" force for the whole race during wintry hardships. Heaney no longer sticks to a single "voice" as the source of his poetic inspiration; he dramatizes the entire story of an Irish legendary hero and treasures it. In a historical context, Heaney's use of the specific Irish image, "a wild white goose" seems to declare his position as a national bard: not only his poetry would be strictly based on Ireland's past, but also, just as he was "quickened" by the story of heroic figures of the past, his works would "quicken" the later generations.

The birth of a poem is completed only when a poet actually articulates words after a thorough excavation of language. In Sonnet VII, Heaney gives a final touch to the rhythm, sound, and words, building his poetry on "linguistic hardcore" (Curtis 117). His versatile use of old – English poetic devices such as sprung rhythm ("dogger, rockall, Malin, Irish Sea") and poetic kennings ("eel – road, seal – road, keel – road, whale – road") brings him back to the very beginning of English literature in the Anglo – Saxon period. He finds the possibility that language can become the major link between "the most ancient and the most civilized mentality." Here, language turns out to be an empowering factor, a possible ground for reconciliation of any hostilities or conflicts among people because it transcends its current existence. Since, throughout the poem, language stands as an "objective correlative" for the historical accumulation of human consciousness, once the poet's burden of language is unloaded, he feels perfectly free with other poetic elements and enjoys his role as a craftsman of words.

For Heaney, poetic articulation does not remain an activity of the moment: it is rather an externalization of long-preserved reality. The deeper the "pith" of culture and tradition from which language is drawn, the stronger influence it exerts on the poetic transformation. For this reason, when Heaney actually articulates the phrase, "A Haven," it becomes a reality with substantial effect: "The word[s] deepening, clearing, like the sky/Elsewhere on Minches, Cromarty, the Faroes." In this climax, the common rural county Wicklow acquires an archytypal status as a "haven" for both the ship and the poet himself.

The last three sonnets illustrate that a poet's command of language is indeed his liberating force and that, by virtue of his contact with latent potentialities of language, the poet's view has widened and his "gaze" expanded. They are developed in free-association of form. Heaney's speculation flows freely from human suffering, to death, and to love. By his thorough exploration of language, he learns how to "fortify the quotidian into work" (Kinahan 411). In the Wasteland-like threat of ugliness and fear depicted in Sonnet IX, Heaney finally experiences an epiphany, a sudden illumination of beauty; he sees "a new moon" in his wife's face: "When I come down, and beyond, your face/*Haunts like a new moon* glimpsed through tangled glass" (emphases added, IX, ll, 13-14). Though fragmentary and indefinite, this transfigured vision moves "beyond" domesticity, and thus, justifies his apology for poetry.

In the last stanza, Heaney is able to transcend even his present existence in a dream-land atmosphere. He joins the legend by associating his wife and himself with the legendary and literary lovers, "Lorenza and Jessica," and "Diarmuid and Grainne." At the same time, he seems to come to terms with several negative aspects of life – an exposure to danger, death, and darkness. Since he has mental space enough to accept various hostile situations as they are, even if the poetic atmosphere gets gloomier and darker, he neither agitates nor anxious. However desolate and lonely his situation might be, he can dream his happiness of their "first night years ago in that hotel/When [his wife] came with [her] deliberate kiss/To raise [them] towards the lovely and painful/Covenants of flesh" (X, ll. 10-13).

The ultimate validity of poetry, however, is not a total exemption from all those dangers. It is only a "respite" and "our [momentary] separateness" (X, ll. 13 – 14) from life's harsh reality. The only justification of the poetic activity is to see "beyond" and provide a vision – however momentary it is – so that one can transcend the reality of the present, still standing on earth. To do so, the poet has to turn to language and dig continuously into its layers hoping that language, by virtue of its abundant potentialities, finally illuminate reality and truth. Indeed, in this process – perhaps, in this process only, his poetic activity becomes a ritual and his poetry finds its place in the literary tradition.

Throughout "Glanmore Sonnets" Heaney records his firm belief in the potentiality of language. He treasures language as far as recovering its original referentiality that goes back to the very beginning of the world in which language perfectly matches with ideas. But in his answer to the efficacy of poetry, Heaney realizes the incompatibility of the poet's sedentary work in the immediate social and political crisis: he shares with Auden the recognition that "poetry makes nothing happen." Nonetheless, as a fugitive poet who, though grown and educated in Belfast, enjoys an idyllic life at Glanmore Castle, he could not remain completely indifferent to the sectarian turbulence in Northern Ireland. Because he was not participating more directly in the struggle of his people, he might have felt feelings of guilt, despair, and responsibility – perhaps, too much to remain reticent. As Perkins points out, in this sequence, he "did not fail to accuse himself of an evasion as his imagination withdrew into the past, but poetry was deepened" (483) due to his serious speculations on the poet's role and the efficacy of language as an illuminator of the poet's creative activity. His reaffirmation of the power of language and his honest evaluation of the limitations and scope of the poetic force prepare him for a new stage in which he can articulate truth and valiantly confront whatever harsh realities. He may now be ready to perform "the poet's double responsibility to tell a truth as well as to make things" with confidence.

< Works Cited >

Bedient, Calvin. "The Music of What Happens." *Parnasus*, 8 (Fall/Winter 1979): 109 – 22.

Curtis, Tony. "A More Social Voice: *Field Work*." *The Art of Seamus Heaney*. Bridgend, Mild Glamorgen: Poetry Wales Press, 1982.

Ellmann, Richard & Robert O'Clair Eds. *The Norton Anthology of Modern Poetry*. New York & London: W. W. Norton & Co; 1988.

Heaney, Seamus. *Field Work*. London: Faber & Faber, 1979.

Kinahan, Frank. "Artists on Art: an Interview with Seamus Heaney." *Critical Inquiry*, 8 (Autumn 1981 – Summer 1982): 405 – 14.

Morrison, Blake. *Seamus Heaney*. London & New York: Metheun, 1982.

Parini, Jay. "Seamus Heaney The Ground Possessed." *Southern Review*, 16 (Winter 1979): 100 – 23.

Perkins, David. *A History of Modern Poetry: Modernism & After*. Cambridge & London: Harvard Univ. Press, 1987.

Samuels, Alix J. *The "Glanmore Sonnets": A Reading and Analysis*. Ann Arbor, MI: Univ. Microfilms International, 1985.

Williams, John. "British Poetry Since 1945: Poetry & the Historical Moment." *Encyclopaedia of Literature and Criticism*. London: Routledge, 1991.

III - 3. Anxiety of Communication in Browning's Dramatic Monologue,
"Bishop Blougram's Apology"

Robert Browning's dramatic monologue technique is a show case of his
anxiety of communication. It is an expression of his own anxiety of
communication and at the same time, a solution to his such anxiety. The
very fact that he incorporates a silent auditor in the poem to whom a
conscious speaker always turns for approval, persuasion, or reprimand
against reveals Browning's anxiety of effective communication. But at the
same time, by securing a listener in the poem, Browning also provides an
answer to such anxiety.

In his 1984 book entitled *Robert Browning: His Poetry and His Audience*, Lee
Erickson mentions Browning's life - long obsession with the problem of
communication and his consequent search for a responsive audience. He
claims that Browning imagined an ideal audience that was intimately aware
of and capable of returning the poet's offered sympathy, and that the one
earthly audience for Browning was Elizabeth, his lover and colleague, and
beyond that, God. He concludes that until Browning wrote *Men and Women*,
he had not discovered an appropriate poetic mode for addressing an audience
and that, after Elizabeth's death, he became more and more self-indulgent,
supposing that no audience really mattered except God.

Along with Erickson's emphasis on Browning's psychological preoccupation
with the intimate and responsive auditor, Ekbert Faas' interdisciplinary
approach to the dramatic monologue (in his 1987 book entitled *Retreat into
the Mind*) opens a psychological or clinical definition of the auditor in the

poem. Tracing a parallel development between the emergence of mental science and of the dramatic monologue in the Nineteenth Century England, Faas compares the poet to the alienist who, through his sympathetic imagination, listens to the patients' innermost thoughts as therapeutic treatment of mental illnesses. He further contends that with the independent activity of listening, the auditor is credited with the same alienist's role by his patient listening to the eccentric and often psychologically abnormal speaker's oration, only to help the latter unburden his emotional and psychological disturbances.

Indeed, Browning's entire poetic career is characterized by his continuous efforts to find a new technique that would fit his poetic objective and to communicate his poetic vision. As a solution, through his dramatic monologue technique, he incorporates auditor figures in his poems and endows them with crucial roles. The development of his auditors takes several stages of emergence, activation, and sophistication. In his earlier poems from *Pauline* to *Pippa Passes,* where Browning's consciousness is rendered rather than the speaker's personality, the auditor figures assume characteristics inherently amorphous, oscillating, and ambiguous profile. Portrayed in ambiguously vacillating characteristics, Pauline, Aprile, Sebald and Ottima all indicate the speaker's (or the poet's) inner states of mind. Meanwhile, in accordance with his focus on the speaker's personality, Browning's later dramatic monologues feature more individualized, particularized, and distinctive auditors, thus, increasing intersubjectivity between a more objectified speaker and a more individualized auditor.

Among his dramatic monologues, the casuistic poems represented by

"Bishop Blougram's Apology" display an acute dramatic tension between the extremely sophisticated speaker and equally opinionated auditor. Though written in the same period as "Andrea del Sarto" and "Fra Lippo Lippi," "Bishop Blougram's Apology" bears several conspicuous marks that command a special treatment. Presenting highly sophisticated interplay, this poem dramatizes the clash of the will between the speaker and the auditor which is "almost Nietzschean" (McGowan 161). In the poem, the speaker's casuistry often jeopardizes the poeticality and makes the poem "perilously near the absence of poetry" (Brooke 394). In addition to its main divergence from other dramatic monologue poems by its departure from the Renaissance and Italian setting and characters towards the contemporary setting and topic, this poem dramatizes the extent to which the intensity of tension and antagonism between the speaker and the auditor provide either resource or impasse to the poet's anxiety of communication, while rendering the auditor's poetic substantiality.

The first step in measuring Browning's substantial anxiety of communication is to understand the considerable degree to which Browning depends on poetic realism in creating his fictional world. One aspect of poetic realism appears as a unique dependence of the poem upon verisimilitude. Compared to the dramatic monologues such as "My Last Duchess" and "Fra Lippo Lippi," this poem incorporates poetic plausibility to the extent that the represented text emerges, as a rupture, from on-going reality, being retrieved, externalized, and concentrated on the speaker Blougram's self-vindicative speech. Defining the dramatic monologue in terms of the retrieval of a part of the speaker's "internal dialogue," J. H. Miller provides a supportive observation:

> Many of his so-called dramatic monologues···. are really
> internal dialogues.··· The only thing certain is that the inner
> dialogue will go on indefinitely, only arbitrarily brought to a
> conclusion, and chopped off into a poem.
>
> *(Disappearance of God* 87)

The reader meets only the minimal portion of the iceberg, but through such a short encounter, he comes to experience the entire world of the poetic characters.

The unique interdependence between the poetic mode and reality generates another aspect of poetic realism which is rhetorical as well as psychological. It is pertinent to the auditor Gigadibs' pre-poetic role which initiates the poetic movement and incessantly enters the speaker's consciousness and oration. More specifically, the poem starts to take its shape by Gigadibs' charge against the Bishop's professional integrity as a spiritual leader. And this pre-poetic text brings about and explains the difference that this poem manifests in comparison to the other dramatic monologues.

As the poetic auditor, Gigadibs outgrows the role of the passive respondent. Bearing an acute polarity to the speaker in terms of his notion of belief and skepticism, he preconditions the poetic context, without which the poem loses its ground of existence. Such initiative action makes the poetic situation extraordinarily compelling and plausible. In turn, expanding the text into the realm of reality, the auditor's primordial text endows the poem with the reciprocity, continuity, and fluidity necessary to create the sense of an on-going debate or a panel discussion. Setting the tone for relations between the two characters, such a pre-poetic act serves as the speaker's working text, an operational center for the speaker to react against, to counterattack, and to modify and revise in order to establish his own. In need of explaining and vindicating himself, Bishop Blougram tries to convince Gigadibs that belief is worthwhile for this worldly comfort and that he is not so despicable a figure as Gigadibs thinks he is. Itself unformed, the extra-poetic substance shapes the pattern of the poetic argument and determines its direction. Through such provision of the pre - poetic text, Browning replaces the arbitrariness and self-motivating impulsiveness of the speaker's utterance with acute dramatic tension and a compelling sense of inevitability, necessity, and psychological urgency.

Apparently, Gigadibs' poetic status is established through a three – stage formation, ranging from his pre - poetic role, through his continuing influence upon the speaker's main argument, to his completion of the poetic action conveyed by the epilogue. His solidity as the auditor lies not only in the continuity of his involvement in the main argument, but also in the scope and range of his influence as its shaping force. It is not sheer exaggeration to say that the poetic action is initiated by Gigadibs, progresses with his constant engagement as the underlying controlling power, and ends with his decisive acting out of his will. Gigadibs' irresistible poetic presence indeed works as a penetrating principle that activates the organism of poetry and forms its full circle of action.

Browning's challenge as a *dramatic poet* reaches its climax with this poem.

Browning reverses the order of the experiments in his early works such as *Paracelsus* and *Pippa Passes* in which he transforms the conventional drama into the dramatic monologue. Upon the basic structure of the dramatic monologue, Browning now launches a drama of the clash of wills between the speaker and the auditor. If he pursues psychological depth and internal probings of human action in *Paracelsus*, he focuses on dramatic plausibility, topical contemporaneity, and intellectual polarity between the two characters in this poem.

Browning stretches the dramatic monologue to its maximum capacity and estimates the poetic weight of each constituting element. On the one hand, allowing full license to the speaker's exclusive right to speak, he subordinates such poetic license to the speaker's consciousness of the auditor. This is certainly designed to stress the substantiality and particularity of the auditor's poetic presence. On the other hand, in order to secure the causality within the dramatic monologue convention, Browning resuscitates the auditor's function to the extent that his silence does neither inhibit, nor paralyze, but rather promotes his power to react. In his interaction with the speaker, the auditor plays a crucial part similar to that of a character in a novel. Meanwhile, Browning portrays the speaker in his close contiguity that the speaker is frequently identified as Browning himself in his verbal expressiveness, his awareness and appropriation of the dramatic monologue convention, and his erudition and intellectual power.

Such expansion of the dramatic monologue poses a concomitant test of Browning's ability as a poet who is restless for proper communication. In the poem in which his intellectual faculty couples with his emotional sensibility, Browning has to keep an acrobatic balance between the lyricism and the "aridity of gray argument" (Raymond 129). His philosophical inquiry is to be pursued without sacrificing concrete elements that communicate the poeticality and lyricism. In addition, the logical continuity of the speaker's argument should be preserved without ruptures or breaks that conversation necessarily entails. Likewise, colloquial vividness and vital interaction between poetic characters must be maintained without hindering the logical reasoning that the seriousness of the topic requires.

Ostensibly, Browning attempts an anatomy of Victorian religious society by means of the speaker's elaborate speech about the nature and use of belief. It registers a one-sided argument addressed by a highly materialistic prelate, Sylvester Blougram, to a literary journalist, Gigadibs. A more psychological approach, however, shows that this poem is equally related to the nineteenth – century intellectual's internal conflict between an extremist position which endorses a "whole faith, or none" (l. 598) attitude and a relative and compromising reception of religion based upon "the fruit it bears" (l. 609). To a certain extent, Blougram's reasoning comprises both of these aspects. It may after all be Blougram himself who is "torn psychologically between opposing forces [such as belief and uncertainty, and strength and weakness], to both of which he owes some allegiance" (King 78).

The interpretive variability has direct relevance to determining the position of the poetic auditor, Gigadibs. Ever since F. E. L. Priestley articulated the long-neglected Gigadibs' primal importance in the poem as one who "dictate[s] its whole course" (168), a persistent division has existed regarding his poetic identity and function. According to Priestley, Roma

King, David Shaw and R. G. Collins, Gigadibs, a thirty-year-old journalist working for *Blackwood's,* is a rare challenger to Blougram's life style as an ecclesiastical leader. For the first time among Browning's auditors, Gigadibs is referred to as an "antagonist" (Thomas 167), a strong "Opponent" (Priestley 169, Shaw 207), a "caviler" (l. 998), and an intractable adversary and enemy. The poetic interpretation accordingly presumes an even-matched tension between the two egos, the speaker and the auditor, which McGowan properly termed (in lieu of "Mr. Sludge, 'the Medium'") as the clash between Nietzschean will-powers (161). Meanwhile, more recent critics such as David Ewbank, Susan Gilhead, and Thomas Fisher contend that Gigadibs is Blougram's *Doppelganger*, an emblem of Blougram's own discomforting voice of skepticism and unbelief. Identifying him as Blougram's younger, more ideal, and "unrealized best self" (118), Fisher interprets the poem as Blougram's "ghost-dialogue" with himself. On the same ground, Ewbank claims that "the conversation between Blougram and Gigadibs is not an exchange between two debaters, but the illusion of dialogue that a ventriloquist creates with his puppet" (260).

Such a polemical contrast is in part modulated in Park Honan's eclectic position in which Gigadibs has both particularly individualistic and generally representative qualities. According to Honan, Gigadibs is simultaneously an independent individual with his own predilections and prejudices, "a representative of mid-nineteenth century intellectual thought-sometimes as the whole age itself" (159), and "the embodiment of the Bishop's own doubts that have been nurtured by the age" (160). On the part of the Bishop, the difficulty arises as much from a casual young man's criticism that tries to "oppugn" his life as from his confrontation with "an integral element of his own character: his own doubting intellectuality" (Honan 160).

Honan's position, in spite of its final proclivity to subordinate the auditor to the speaker, is comprehensively illuminating and to the point. For, such an intricate relationship between Gigadibs and Blougram elucidates the complexity, ambiguity, and disparity of the psychological and rhetorical movement of the poem, while pushing the poetic challenge to the extreme. By maintaining the duality of Gigadibs' poetic identity, Honan introduces a double challenge to Blougram's rhetoric. In this scheme, Blougram has to beat his opponent, Gigadibs – a reminder of the uncertain and largely skeptical mass; at the same time, he has to reaffirm his value system by winning the reality within – the internal voice of his conscience, his presiding self embodied by Gigadibs. While distinguishing Gigadibs from other auditors in Browning's other dramatic monologues, such an observation helps locate Gigadibs on a dialectical center. In Gigadibs, various functions and identities of the auditors from earlier poems, such as Aprile, Festus, Lucrezia, and the Police chieftain, are culminated and synthesized. More precisely, Gigadibs evolves from these precedent auditors as a fully-developed character.

In such complex interlocking between the speaker and the auditor, the term 'sophistication' may be applicable, and it not only presupposes Gigadibs' compatibility to a speaker who is as intellectually armed and rhetorically sophisticated as Bishop Blougram, but it also implies his contribution to the otherwise internalized and complicated poetic situation.

In fact, the constituting elements are so inextricably interdependent that, by claiming "the sophistication of the auditor," we have to undergo the labyrinth of critical controversies in which most Browning scholars have been involved. He might possibly run a risk of adding more questions to the already knotty poem. In order to establish the auditor's poetic status, he has to determine his interpretive position in regard to the authenticity of the epilogue of the poem, the credibility of Gigadibs' opinion as attributed by Blougram, and the consequent reliability of Blougram's personality as the poetic speaker, and further his sincerity as a human being. Conceivably, one has to come to terms with the following highly ambiguous questions: Is the narrator in the epilogue Browning's mouthpiece or a disembodied voice? That is, is the epilogue an articulation of Browning's authentic position toward his fictional characters? Is Gigadibs' emigration to Australia a manifestation of his blunt refusal to accept Blougram's value system (as Arnold Shapiro, Ian Jack, and Rupert Palmer claim) or of his defeat followed by a reluctant exile (as Priestley and Shaw contend), or of his exploration for a more healthy environment and a more creative way of life (as King contends), or of his search for instant material prosperity and acquisition of wealth (as Collins maintains)? Often the reader has to be involved in a rather precarious situation: he has to trust Gigadibs' opinion as expressed in Blougram's words, while rejecting Blougram's view of the nature and use of belief, not to mention his personality, as insincere and self-servingly distorted.

Noticeably, the very core of critical debates about Bishop Blougram has been the same matter of deciding the authority and authenticity of the text, morally as well as rhetorically. Scholars have questioned the reliability of Blougram as the poetic speaker, his sincerity as a person, the acceptability and sobriety of his view of belief and conduct, and of Gigadibs' position, the degree of his involvement in his fictional world, and the credibility and implication of the poetic epilogue. In their efforts to match Blougram and Gigadibs to the historical prototypes, they are even concerned about the veracity of the poetic characters compared to their original models.

Ironically, such fervid interest in poetic authenticity has generated an unprecedented critical incongruity. Taken by the Bishop's eloquent oration, earlier critics such as Priestley have completely ignored the poetic epilogue. Recently, doubting scholars have consistently expressed skepticism as to the reliability of Blougram and the authenticity of his argument, while accepting, perhaps too easily and readily, the poetic epilogue as an articulation of Browning's final attitude towards his characters. If the earlier position is wrong for its total disregard of an important portion of the poem (i. e. the epilogue), the recent enthusiasm exclusive to the epilogue is also mistaken because the narrator's explicit antagonism against Blougram cannot be the only standard for crediting the epilogue with authenticity and discrediting the main body of argument.

A welcome corrective to such a maze of critical inconsistency is given by Sarah Gilhead. In an article entitled "'Read the Text Right': Textual Strategies in 'Bishop Blougram's Apology'" (1986), Gilhead interprets the poem in terms of an elaborate game of reading in which the characters' articulations from disfigurative or revisionary readings of the prior texts established either by other characters or by their own narrations. She views the poem as a chain of rhetorical "revisions and rejections of, reactions and responses to" (53) the previous texts, the claimant of which shifts from Gigadibs, to Blougram, to the narrator, and to the reader. This view, while liberating the text from any dictatorial authenticity of one element, lays the groundwork for establishing Gigadibs' position as a tenable one equivalent to Blougram's.

For the time being, such disengagement of the text allows the reader to discount not only the distinction between the speaker and the auditor, but also the advantage of the speaker's exclusive right to speech and the potential disadvantage of the auditor's silence. Paradoxically, this suspension of the dramatic monologue activates its very dynamics. No sooner is its operation discontinued than we see the emergence of what Ricks mentions as the tension between strong speech and strong silence, opening our vision to new vistas of interactions between the speaker and the auditor.

Previously ignored, the speaker's inordinate consciousness of the auditor's poetic presence, the heavy pressure imposed on the speaker, his suppressed hostility, his consequent intentionality, and his stipulated manipulation may now be exposed. The situation is intensified by Blougram's disconcerted self-proclamation that Gigadibs despises him. Whether he argues on Gigadibs' premise or on Christian ground, Blougram's discussion revolves around his hurt pride coming from such self-consciousness. This baffling awareness stands as "the [Bishop's] strongest rallying point" (Shaw 214): it starts and ends his argument, forming a rhetorical circle. It seems evident that, in such a circular construction, the argument remains trapped and stands still. A crucial clue is offered by Blougram's final remarks in which he asks Gigadibs "To discontinue – not detesting, not/Defaming, but at least – despising me!" (ll. 969-970). The message is that he would not mind Gigadibs "detestation" or "defamation," unless Gigadibs "despises" him. The difference between the words in these two groups is, as R. G. Collins remarks, "one of ego" (7), which again is etymological and psychological. The terms, "detestation" and "defamation" are ordinarily applied to the social impact brought in originally by the difference or opposition of opinions or positions. But the term, "to despise" is more adequately applied to a devaluation, degradation, and humiliation of one's self-esteem as a human being. It is to regard someone as "worthless" (*Longman Dictionary of Contemporary English* 298). Without doubt, it leaves a deeper scar upon the accused than "detestation" or "defamation," and thus requires more conscious effort to restore than it otherwise might have done.

As the Bishop's overriding concern, his excessive sensitivity to the impression he makes upon his social inferior, Gigadibs, reflects and is reflected by his rhetorical anguish and anxiety in which he constantly imagines what Gigadibs would reply to his oration [e. g. "You'll reply" (l. 1340), "You'll say" (ll. 676, 713), "You'd find" (l. 749), etc.]. His desire for Gigadibs' responsiveness is such that it creates a vent in his perverted confidence that Gigadibs respects him and envies his "Status, entourage, [and] worldly circumstance" (l. 26). Blougram even asserts in his imagined conjecture that Gigadibs would "turn [his dinner with the Bishop] to such capital account" (l. 30), making it "the highest honour in your life, /The thing you'll crown yourself with, all your days" (ll. 916-917).

Beyond doubt Blougram is a masterful rhetoric. His treatment of

Gigadibs rests on his calculated ambivalence between his elevation and deflation of Gigadibs, or more accurately, Blougram's constant effort to establish Gigadibs in a position that is both intellectually and rhetorically compatible with his own takes a double track. On the one hand, he shows an extreme concern for the condition of discussion, that is, the fairness and appropriateness of the situation in which both the speaker and the auditor participate on equal terms. On the other hand, he proclaims his descent to Gigadibs' premise in his argument "I mean to meet you on your own premises:/Good, here go mine in company with yours!" (ll. 171-172). This is certainly Blougram's gesture of concessive assimilation of himself with Gigadibs, except that it turns out to be sheer condescension intent on securing a rhetorical safety-zone.

Blougram's manipulation is obvious from the very first line in which he sets the stage for the discussion: "no more wine? then we' ll push back chairs and talk" (l. 1). Notable in this line is the tension between plural pronoun "we" and the speaker's initiative in setting the time and atmosphere of the argument. It indicates the Bishop's monopolized control carried out in disguised mutuality. In the next stage, this strategy is further advanced. Not only does Blougram create the impression of Gigadibs' equal participation in determining the process of the argument, but he makes it a willing "engagement" agreed upon by two parties: "Beside't is our *engagement*: don't you know,/I *promised*, if you'd watch a dinner out,/*We*'d see truth dawn *together*." He tries to establish Gigadibs in the position that is worth refuting: "So, you *despise* me, Mr. Gigadibs,/*No depreciation*, – nay, *I beg you*, sir!" (emphases added, ll. 13-14). Tinged with histrionic flattery, the tone of the quoted sentence is openly humiliating and mockingly satirical.

Blougram manifests himself to be a traditionalist, an institutionalist, and an adherent to the established convention, far exceeding Gigadibs, the narrator in the epilogue, and probably, even most of the readers. This is most remarkable in his "extra-fictive consciousness" (Christopher J. Rogers viii) in which, as Langbaum notes, "he has one foot inside the poem and one foot outside" (204). More specifically, Blougram, a poetic character, endeavors to authenticate the generic condition of the dramatic monologue form. While entertaining and fortifying his license to speak – "such as you know me, I am free to say" (l. 310) – he justifies the auditor's silence in terms of a "fair" exchange of speech rights: "It's fair give and take:/You have had your turn and spoken your home-truths:/The hand's mine now, and here you follow suit" (ll. 46-48).

The progress of Blougram's argument rests on the principle of dichotomy. The way he handles the issue is indeed extraordinarily skillful and suspiciously purposeful. In the main, he depends on over-simplification of the issue by means of dichotomy. He schematizes the rather intricate and subtle matter of belief vs. unbelief in a way that the speaker and the auditor each represents one side of the categorized opinions and ideas. For instance, as Raymond explicates, "Blougram widens the chasm between belief and reason in two directions. If the maximum of belief is represented by an absolute form of it in Roman Catholicism, the maximum of agnosticism [is represented] by a complete intellectual scepticism" (119). Then, as King believes, Blougram pushes Gigadibs "to commit himself to an extreme position and then to turn his argument against his in the form of a countercharge" (87). Not only does he dichotomize whatever issue he handles, but also he repeatedly attributes "the privileged terms [for himself], while reserving for Gigadibs unprivileged terms" (Gilhead 55). Blougram's oversimplification, as an easy means of appropriating Gigadibs' position, helps effectuate his self-vindication, but at the cost of his honest self-scrutiny.

Such manipulation of the issue perfectly fits the Bishop's dichotomized view of the world in which people are divided into two groups, the Carlylean heroes and the hero-worshippers (Susan H. Aiken 31-33), the Bishops and the "rough purblind mass we seek to rule" (l. 756), and the winners and the losers. In his reasoning based on the standard of material prosperity and complacency, the Bishop himself supercedes the literary hero (Shakespeare), the political hero (Napoleon), and the religious theorist (Strauss) except for Luther. His main strategy is to demolish one by one the historically-esteemed figures in a way that deprives Gigadibs of the ground to base his opinions upon.

In fact, Blougram's keen consciousness of Gigadibs' power to "protest" and the accompanying anxiety control his rhetoric so much that they preclude the otherwise extensive speculation on the issue at hand and on himself. His rhetoric is built around a set of fragmentary ideas and notions of belief and scepticism, most of which, improvised for "argumentatory purposes" (l. 993), are represented as "fixtures" (l. 986). This is evidenced by Blougram's multifarious and off-handed use of metaphors and similes. A representative example of his arbitrary improvisation of metaphor is found in his argument for "[a life] of faith diversified by doubt" (l. 211) over "a life of doubt diversified by faith" (l. 210). In order to illustrate his point, he invents a metaphor of the "way over the mountain" (l. 198). Noticeable is the way in which an accidental articulation of the word "way" functions as a cue for improvising the metaphor of the "way over the mountain." To a large extent, the entire operation of the metaphor depends on a chain of echoing sounds, from "some way," through "The way, the Truth, the Life," to "that way/Over the mountain":

> If so, when, where and how? *some way* must be, –
> One feel about, and soon or late you hit
> Some sense, in which it might be, after all.
> Why not, '*The Way, the Truth, the Life*?'
> > > > *– that way*
> Over the mountain, which who stands upon
> Is apt to doubt if it be meant for a road;
> While, if he views it from the waste itself,
> Up goes the line there, plain from base to brow,
> Not vague, mistakable! what's a break or two
> Seen from the unbroken desert either side?
> > > (emphases added, ll. 194-203).

As Blougram himself says, the presented metaphor registers how "some way must be, – – Once feel about, and soon or late you hit/Some sense, in which it might be, after all" (ll. 194-196). Technically ingenious though his recording of the cognitive/creative process, it renders the arbitrariness and contingency, rather than the necessary credibility and sincerity, upon which Blougram's argument is built. Likewise, instead of bearing his confidence and assurance, Blougram's garrulity accelerates the poetic speed and intensifies the sense of urgency, desperation, and uneasiness involved in his self-defense.

The Bishop's display of "sophisticated self-consciousness" (Slinn 61) qualifies the rhetorical aim, restrains the scope of the argument, and cripples the poetic development. Blougram's speech, far from being "a systematic defense of faith" (Shaw 213), does not present much substantial progress. His protest/defense based on his emotional injury blocks the progress of the argument and keeps his deepest self untouched. Unmistakably, Blougram's every effort veers to reiterating the same story in slightly varied versions until it squares with his exorbitant pursuit of worldly power. For Blougram, such verbalized consciousness is modified into a valid excuse for a deliberate inhibition from confronting the core of the matter, "the issue of spiritual realization" (Slinn 61). From the beginning, Blougram obscures whatever is Gigadibs' actual challenge by accentuating the sentiments that he thinks Gigadibs personally holds about him. His frequent repetition of, and return to, "the first fact" (l. 49) and "the starting place" (l. 144) belongs to the same conscious act that allows him to deviate from an opportunity for a more sincere and honest self – confrontation.

The Bishop's *argumentum ad absurdium* appears most obvious in his use of the figure of speech. The most predominant and most noticeable fallacy in this provision is his degradation of lofty themes by means of a bathetic use of the metaphor, which is intensified by his proclivity to measure spiritual value in terms of "the fruit it bears" (l. 609). Particularly open to criticism is his use of the cabin image:

How we may lead a comfortable life,
How suit our luggage to the cabin's size.

Of course you are remarking all this time
How narrowly and grossly I view life,
Respect the creature – comforts, care to rule
The masses, and regard complacently
'The cabin,' in our old phrase. Well, I do.
I act for, talk for, live for this world now,
As this world prizes action, life and talk:
(emphases added, ll. 762-770).

By using the image of 'cabin,' he confines the passage of human life to a material condition (e. g. "snug and well-appointed *berth* like mine" (emphasis added)) and "what might be" to "what is" (l. 346). For him, only the accommodation en route makes an ideal journey; neither the motivation, nor the direction, nor the destination of the journey matters.

That he is prone to figurative speech evidences his intellectual power, possibly featuring him as "a man of reason, practical and realistic" (Slinn 60). What detracts from this extraordinary ability is the way in which it is exploited sheerly to emphasize his worldly success and power. Versatile and multifarious, images he employs are the very means of bathos by which he denigrates the otherwise elevating and lofty theme into triviality, the fundamental and essential into contingent and peripheral, and the spiritual and abstract into tangible and incidental. At the same time, they contribute to "evad[ing] his inner life, the prospect of emotional and spiritual reality" (Slinn 60). Just like the monks' comprehension of soul in terms of "fire, smoke,· · · vapour done up like a new – born babe" (ll. 184-185) in "Fra Lippo Lippi", Blougram's metaphorical grasp of spiritual reality is insubstantial and degrading. His undue concern with this world and its value renders him no less egocentric than non-believers who are afraid of committing themselves to any objects of belief.

Intriguingly purposeful, Blougram's intentionality provides an index to measure Gigadibs' irresistible poetic presence, Blougram's compulsory perception of Gigadibs and his role, and consequently the tension between the two. Undoubtedly, the Bishop shows a more advanced social consciousness than that of any speakers in Browning's early poems. Far superior to any other speakers (e. g. Andrea del Sarto, the dying Bishop, and even the Duke of Ferrara), he struggles to instill a good impression in Gigadibs who he believes envies his worldly influence. He proclaims his concession in which he argues on Gigadibs' premise at the beginning and consistently returns to that position. He is certainly much more sophisticated and better aware of the importance of the auditor's poetic equality than other earlier monologuists. Being nourished through his professional performance, the bishop's social consciousness, however, operates under the assumption that the elevation of his opponent's position is not to degrade, but to elevate his own. Blougram acknowledges that it is a necessary means of his self-aggrandizement, of the fulfillment of his egocentric desires.

It is in such effort, however, that a double irony is superimposed and finally takes over the poetic meaning. Blougram's choice of a concessive position in which he argues from Gigadibs premise contributes to revealing his very nature, which seek "power, peace, pleasantness and length of days" (l. 237) and hungers for "the creature-comforts" (l. 766), rather than persuading Gigadibs. More crucial to the poetic effect is yet another layer of irony derived from the first irony. It is the discrepancy between Blougram's inadvertent self-revelation and his inability to comprehend such a situation. He creates the poetic irony without recognizing it and, more seriously, without learning from it. Apart from his self-addressed incompatibility to "those exceptional/And privileged great natures that dwarf mine" (ll. 934-935), his *virtual* inability to be a self-ironist causes the stagnation of the poetic development (emphasis added). His ultimate problem lies in the incongruity between the speciousness of his self-knowledge and his actual inability to grow, to participate in "the evolution of successive spheres" (l. 786) through "ever trying to be and ever being" (l. 785).

In conjunction with such disparity, ambivalence, and irony in the Bishop's rhetoric, Browning's imposition of a double subtlety in which the Bishop engages in the argument on the premise of his public role should not be slighted. The publicity which locates him in a socially influential place betokens his vulnerability in accepting his innermost self. After all, his public-oriented argumentation endorses and often encourages his double removal from reality, hence determining the quality of his self-understanding, and further the resolution of the poem. As Slinn mentions, "through focusing on the reality without, [Blougram] is not required to confront the reality within" (60). At stake in such a case is his earnest self-illumination. If he perversely engages in double talk or deliberate self-delusion, he becomes double removed from reality – one from legitimately predominant ideas and general perspectives, and the other from his essential self hence a double difficulty of his honest self-scrutiny. Robert Garratt's notion of the "double mask," in this sense, seems to find its most illustrative example in the casuistic speakers.

Blougram's resistance to growth and change might be viewed as a reflection of the difficulty of conversion. Resorting to a self-sufficient world which includes networks of believers and priests, Blougram does not even try to bring changes upon his life: "I'm at ease now, friend; worldly in this world,/I take and like its way of life" (ll. 797-798). Although he is aware of "how narrowly and grossly [he] views life" (l. 765), the tone betrays such awareness and his ultimate complacency vitiates his desire for change. For a reason different from Andrea's, but as strong as Andrea, the Bishop sticks to the status quo. As he himself says to Gigadibs, "If I prefer remaining my poor self,/I say so not in self-dispraise but praise" (ll. 495-496). His "business is not to remake [him]self,/But make the absolute best of what God made" (ll. 354-355).

If the earlier monologuists' solipsistic view of the self impedes their relationship with their auditors, Bishop Blougram's excessive conformity to his public role poses the same danger of inhibiting a sound development of inter-subjectivity. The Bishop contrasts sharply to the earlier monologuists such as the Duke of Ferarra and Andrea del Sarto in that he is too absorbed in his social role which, in fact, is nothing but a camouflaged egocentricity. Though he shows an advanced social consciousness upon claiming his argument on Gigadibs' premise, his ultimate directive nullifies such concession as ego-oriented.

The Bishop's appropriation of his public position for his egocentric fulfillment is most apparent in his disclosed reason for choosing the ecclesiastical profession. Not only does he understand belief in terms of worldly wisdom, but, for him, the motive and effect of his bishopric is reversed. While insisting that belief is a matter of willful choice, he confides that he "happened to be born in" (l. 302) Catholicism and took his bishopric as nothing more than the "best and readiest means of living by" (l. 304). It serves as an effective means of satisfying "the power in me and will to dominate/Which I must exercise, they hurt me else" (ll. 322-323) and "exalt[ing] me o'er my fellows in the world/And mak[ing] my life an ease and joy and pride" (ll. 317-318).

The undisclosed proportion of the potential threat and intimidation that Gigadibs imposes upon the Bishop might, though only in part, legitimize Blougram's strong adherence to the present state. What immediately matters to Blougram is to win over his opponent, Gigadibs, even prior to exerting any effort to review his notion of belief and himself. According to Ewbank, engrossed in his self-imposed pressure to beat Gigadibs, Blougram is busy with demolishing Gigadibs' position, rather than constructing a logically infallible argument (260). In the same way that the anonymous Bishop's imminent death (in "The Bishop Orders His Tomb at St. Praxed's Church") both incites and restrains his effort for self-understanding, Gigadibs here serves as simultaneously the path and the impasse to Blougram's self-scrutiny. Initially, by questioning the integrity of his role in performing his ecclesiastical profession, Gigadibs elicits Blougram's urgent need for self-defense, while engendering his possible self-introspection. At the same time, Gigadibs' charge stimulates Blougram's instinct for self-protection and the subsequent withdrawal from whatever effort Blougram could have made for self-search. Here, Blougram's consciousness of Gigadibs as a "caviler" (l. 998) that needs to be beaten outweighs his effort for self-understanding: he recoils on his social self which is, in worldly terms, far superior to Gigadibs' and arms himself with it.

The ambivalence of Gigadibs' poetic function might in part be responsible for the prevailing critical confusion, while openly and intricately engaging the reader in the evolution of poetic meaning. To a considerable degree, the critical assessment of this poem rests on each individual's view of the nature and use of faith. In the same way as the Bishop and Gigadibs create a polarity, readers will be divided into two camps. Those who endorse the practicality of faith might take Blougram's compromising posture as a proper means of coming to terms with contemporary society; those who support the absolutist position will certainly consider Gigadibs' charge against Blougram valid. More intriguingly, granted that one accepts Blougram's position, he undergoes oscillation not only between sympathy and judgment, but also between responsiveness and revulsion. As Mermin says, "it takes casuistry almost equal to the speaker's own" (60) to figure out Blougram's character and to decide one's own attitudes toward him. Browning, in this sense, does not offer any fixed text, nor a "firm place [for the reader] to stand, [nor] a stable structure to construct [from]" (Gibson 204). The poem presents various perspectives of faith and unbelief without voicing any authenticity of a certain position. Not only the polarity of the issue, embodied in two poetic characters, but also the degree of Browning's involvement remains ambiguous and opaque until the end of the poem.

It is in such vein that taking Gigadibs' point of view as purely Blougram's fabrication becomes a risky assumption. Not only does it weaken the dramatic tension, but it also disavows the poetic details applied to Gigadibs. In the poem, Gigadibs is a particular individual with clear opinions based on his specific perspective, intellectual sensibility, and reasoning ability. He is not a lightweight opponent to the Bishop. Although Blougram avoids an accurate rendition of Gigadibs' original charges against him, the textual obscurity serves all the more to fortify the density and power of the blow Gigadibs inflicts upon Blougram.

What should be clarified here is the distinction between Blougram's morality and his rhetorical effectuality. Although Blougram exploits Gigadibs' position through his exclusive right of speech, Gigadibs' undeniable individuality is still maintained. This is evinced even by Blougram's specific and detailed rendition of Gigadibs' reactions, responses, and opinions, which encompass direct quotations, conjectural or imagined quotations and narration, description of gestures or expressions, and paraphrases of Gigadibs' words. It we disregard such specific details as morally invalid just because they are sheerly the product of Blougram's wit and conceit, then we might likely be to repudiate the fictionality of the created world, which, in turn, leads to a total rejection of the poem itself. Of course, I do not insist that we have to take whatever Blougram imputes to Gigadibs. Acknowledging that Blougram ingeniously exploits and insinuates Gigadibs' points of view, we should distinguish the solidity of Gigadibs' poetic status from the misappropriation of his opinions by the Bishop.

Furthermore, it is the specificity and vividness of Blougram's description of Gigadibs' position that bears irresistible testimony to the substantiality and concreteness of the poetic world, which, in turn, serves to maintain the tension, tight and even – matched between two strong powers.

The presented perspective is, nevertheless, not unattended by Browning's own view, and this explains the unusual critical confusion and controversy over the poem. Norton Crowell notes, though in reserved terms, that "Blougram's argument is not markedly inconsistent with Browning's known anti-asceticism, love of good living, and faith in the function of doubt as a text" (198). In particular, several passages in which Blougram bursts into impulsive lyricism (e. g. the passages about the necessity of faith and about the interdependence between faith and doubt) are indicative of Browning's notion of certain aspects of belief. What undermines their credibility is the way Blougram misapplies originally well-intended intuitive passages and religious ideas to his egoistic purposes. Blougram is ready not only to "sa[y] true things but call them by wrong names" (l. 996) but also to distort Browning's ideas "until they mean much the opposite of their religious intent" (Crowell 201). Within the poetic context, the ultimate function of those lyrical passages becomes at best dubious and egocentric, drawn to justify Blougram's worldly success.

If Blougram's proclaimed concession of arguing on Gigadibs' premise indicates the extent to which he manipulates the poetic situation, Browning's incorporation of additional perspective through the epilogue reveals the limitation of such manipulative tactics. To a certain extent, a main controversy about "Bishop Blougram" perpetuates the interpretation of this portion in which a narrator intrudes in seemingly authorial voice. In terms of the dramatic monologue technique, the existence of this post – script might easily be construed as superfluity. A well – meant justification might be that, with the dramatic monologue mode, Browning could not accommodate his message effectively, thus inevitably interpolating the additive explication through the epilogue. As Hoxie Fairchild maintains, "Browning the psychologist may need Browning the moralist" (221). If not Fairchild, one with a similar view would think at best that, with these superfluous lines, Browning intends to compensate whatever unskillful workmanship he commits in his application of the dramatic monologue to a highly intellectual issue.

Persuasive though it is, such a position easily lends itself to the conclusion that this narrative is thus Browning's "artistic flaw" (Jack 206). It presupposes not only an absence or fallibility of Browning's plan for the poem but also the paucity and ineffectuality of his revision, which is not true. On the contrary, Browning painstakingly revised the manuscript several times and never thought of this poem as a negligible product of improvisation (Rogers 163-164).

In order to do more justice to Browning's meticulous construction of the poem, this epilogue should be seen from other interpretive points of view, for instance, in its contribution to enrichment of poetic perspectives and the overall scope that the poem encompasses. Or, perhaps, it embodies Browning's misgivings of being pre-empted by his fictional speaker who has grown unacceptably closest to him among monologuists in his "extra – fictive" ability represented in his understanding and abuse of the dramatic monologue convention.

While tantalizingly attracting, the epilogue baffles the reader with several possibilities that the narrator might be viewed other than either as Browning or as Browning's spokesman. In a strictly neutral sense, the narrator is a disembodied voice who, in his god's eye view, informs the post – poetic situation in which the Bishop comfortably settles in his now – smoothened consciousness and Gigadibs leaves for Australia with settler's implements. In the rhetorical structure of the poem, the narrator might simply be what Sarah Gilhead contends as a claimant for the speech right protesting against the Bishop. The narrator's explicit antagonism against Blougram might be his way of appealing for a usurpation of that right. Or, the narrator might represent a certain reader group who, unpretentiously indignant at Blougram's religious view, censure his worldly exploitation of spiritual leadership. If the poem is interpreted in terms of Blougram's self – confrontation, then, the narrator may embody Blougram's own discomforting voice of honesty and sincerity that is buried deep in his psyche and that, after all his eloquent self-defense, is still unreconciled with his social self. Whatever his identity, it is certain that the narrator emerges as a strong opponent to the Bishop, perhaps, even stronger than Gigadibs.

With such variety of possible identities, the narrator launches major challenges to the authority of the poetic text, the speaker, and the reader. First, the most noticeable and certainly the most immediately relevant to the auditor's poetic status is the narrator's denial of the authenticity of Blougram's argument and the consequent dislocation of the poetic text. His strategy is to attack the Bishop's rhetorical fallibility, lack of authenticity and causality, and contingency of the rhetorical ground. It is directed against Blougram's arbitrary and whimsical construction of the argument. He maintains that Blougram represents certain improvised metaphors and eccentric conceits as "fixtures" (l. 986) for "argumentatory purposes" (l. 982). According to him, unable to reach the "hell – deep instincts" and "not having in readiness/Their nomenclature and philosophy" (ll. 990-995), Blougram could not properly articulate some crucial points: "He said true things, but called them by wrong names" (l. 997). Second, the narrator, while showing explicit antagonism to Blougram, assumes himself to be Gigadibs sympathizer, and even his accomplice in his protest against Blougram. In his final statement, in which he wishfully imagines that Gigadibs now "Has tested his first plough,/And studied his last chapter of St. John" (ll. 1013-1014), the reader even detects a tone of patronizing seniority and affected privity. Nevertheless, his report of the post-argument situation substantiates Gigadibs' reaction in terms of the latter's execution of his potential to resist. Deferring these new perspectives to the reader, the narrator appears as a new authority replacing Blougram's long occupation and eloquent argument and disqualifying his authoritative position.

How far we have to take the narrator's view as Browning's own remains uncertain and depends on each individual, but, with this epilogue, we are relieved from the heavy authenticity that Blougram's text loads us with. The narrator emerges, in this respect, as a liberating force. He introduces a critical spirit revolting against the established authority of the Bishop.

Gigadibs' action-oriented reaction coming from "his sudden healthy vehemence" (l. 1007) indeed stresses his power to resist, to act out his will.

No other poem features the auditor's reaction as unequivocally as this one. It goes beyond his repudiation, by keeping silence, to reply: it is carried out in a specific movement of the geographical locations and professions. In particular, that Gigadibs left for Australia with "settler's implements" rather than "cabin furniture" attests to Gigadibs' long-range vision and fore – sighted respective. Rather than indicating the auditor's loss of speech right or his incompatibility, his silence allows him a space for speculation in a way that provokes him to carry out what he esteems as an ideal style of living. Showing the extent to which the auditor is sophisticated, Gigadibs' such reaction completes the cycle of the poetic action which the auditor has started from outside the poetic text. As Laird points out, whereas "the Bishop is no closer to becoming one of those 'privileged great natures that dwarf mine' at the end of the dinner than he was at the beginning" (308), Gigadibs becomes active, at least "beginning to struggle upward toward his ideal" (308). Gigadibs' action-oriented response has an effect of significantly vitiating the Bishop's superior rhetoric and invalidates his well – organized and meticulously performed argument.

At the same time, Gigadibs' emigration to Australia counter proves the extent to which the Bishop's unresolved conflict between a person and his role stifles his power to act. Blougram himself envisages such internal conflict through the metaphor of an actor who played "Death with pasteboard crown, sham orb and tinselled dart,/And called himself the monarch of the world" (ll. 68-69), only to be touched by Death himself immediately after the performance. The Bishop's dilemma is that his over-conformity to his role paralyzes his power to act, to activate his personality to the full, and that this deprives him of his genuine self from which he can speak sincerely. Too accommodated to his public image, the bishop is incapable of "be[ing] [him]self, imperial, plain and true" (l. 77). Through Blougram, Browning raises a question directed to the existential condition of human beings – whether one's genuine self is ever compatible to his socially cultivated image or role.

The speaker's problem of consistency and sincerity is closely related to the efficacy of language and veracity of verbal articulation. Perhaps, this offers the raison d'etre of the post-script epilogue: through this epilogue, Browning might have wished to convey what Blougram could not represent, i. e. "certain hell-deep instincts" because "man's weak tongue/Is never hold to utter in their truth" (ll. 990-991). Hardly released from the web of Blougram's stipulated intentionality, the verbosity of the poetic argument is after all nothing but a means of concealing the deepest thoughts and the most subtle perceptions that are congenial to his innermost mind.

The embedded irony is then that "the better the speaker controls his words to fit his purpose, the more deceitful he is, and the more estranged from himself" (Mermin 65). Reminiscent of the situation of "My Last Duchess," the Bishop's eloquence is the very proof of his limitation and his defect as a social being.

As a casuistic poem, "Bishop Blougram's Apology" presents a special type of discourse in which the interaction between the speaker and the auditor and between language and truth raises a serious question of verity. In such discourse, the speaker's verbal articulation could not be more fluent, more sophisticated, or more (pseudo)logical, but at the same time, it could also be quite deceptive, delusive, and insincere. Meanwhile, the auditor's silence after a pre - poetic initiative could not be more impotent, but it could also be pregnant with meanings.

In this poem, Browning seems to push the ever-conflicting issues of speech and silence to their maximum edge and measures how far poet's anxiety of communication can be encouraged or disturbed by each activity. Perpetually casting doubt upon the speaker's sincerity as well as the efficacy of verbal expression, Browning transforms such suspicion and uncertainty in the poetic rhetoric into strong evidence for the certainty and fortification of the auditor's potential to resist and further to deflate the speaker. Nevertheless, by presenting irresistible poetic substantiality of the auditor figure, Browning reveals his confidence in communicating his poetic message, while taking a great challenge as a poet who is anxious to get his message across. Through "Bishop Blougram's Apology," Browning may present his own apology as a poet who is anxious to communicate his message to the reader. And by dramatizing two strong figures of the speaker and the auditor, he experiments the extent to which his anxiety of communication is solved.

< Works Cited >

Aiken, Susan Hardy. "Bishop Blougram and Carlyle." *Victorian Poetry*, 16 (1978): 323 – 40.

Bandelin, Carl Frederick. "Browning and the Premises of the Dramatic Monologue." An Unpublished Dissertation. Yale University, 1979.

Brooke, Stopford. *The Poetry of Robert Browning*. London: Isbister and Co; 1902.

Browning, Robert. *Poetical Works 1833 – 1864*. Ed. by Ian Jack. London, Oxford, New York: Oxford Univ. Press, 1975.

Christ, Carol T. *The Finer Optic: The Aesthetic of Particularity in Victorian* Poetry. New Haven and London: Yale Univ. Press, 1975.

Collins, R. G. "Browning's Practical Prelate: the Lesson of 'Bishop Blougram's Apology'." *Victorian Poetry*, 13 (1975): 1 – 20.

Crowell, Norton B. *A Reader's Guide to Robert Browning*. Albuquerque: Univ. of New Mexico Press, 1972.

_____*The Triple Soul: Browning's Theory of Knowledge*. Albuquerque: Univ. of New Mexico Press, 1963.

DeVane, W. Clyde. *A Browning Handbook*. 2nd ed. New York: Appleton – Century – Crofts, 1955.

Dupras, Joseph A. "Reader – Auditor Coordination in Browning's 'A Forgiveness'." *Victorian Poetry*, 27 (1989): 135 – 50.

Erickson, Lee. *Robert Browning: His Poetry and His Audience*. Ithaca & London: Cornell Univ. Press, 1984.

Ewbank, David R. "Bishop Blougram's Argument." *Victorian Poetry*, 10 (1972): 257 – 63.

Faas, Ekbart. *Retreat into the Mind: Victorian Poetry and the Rise of Psychiatry*. Princeton, NJ: Princeton Univ. Press, 1988.

Fairchild, Hoxie E. "Browning the Simple-Hearted Casuist." *University of Toronto Quarterly*, 18 (1949): 234 – 40.

Garrett, Marvin P. "Language and Design in *Pippa Passes*." *Victorian Poetry,* 13 (1975): 47 – 60.

Gibson, Mary Ellis. *History and the Prism of Art: Browning's Poetic Experiments*. Columbus: Ohio State Univ. Press, 1987.

Gilhead, Sarah. 'Read the Text Right': Textual Strategies in "Bishop Blougram's Apology". *Victorian Poetry,* 24 (1986): 47 – 67.

Honan, Park. *Browning's Characters: A Study in Poetic Technique*. New London, Connecticut: Yale Univ. Press, 1969.

King, Roma A. *The Focusing Artifice: The Poetry of Robert Browning*. Athens, Ohio: Ohio Univ. Press, 1968.

Laird, Robert G. "'He did not sit five minutes': The Conversion of Gigadibs." *University of Toronto Quarterly*, 45 (1976): 295 – 313.

Langbaum, Robert W. *The Poetry of Experience: The Dramatic Monologue in Modern Literary Tradition*. New York: Norton, 1963.

Longman Dictionary of Contemporary English. Essex: Longman Group Ltd; 1978.

Mermin, Dorothy. *The Audience in the Poem: Five Victorian Poets*. New Brunswick, NJ: Rutgers Univ. Press, 1983.

Miller, J. Hillis. *The Disappearance of God: Five Nineteenth – Century Writers*. Cambridge, Mass.: The Belknap Press of Harvard Univ; 1963.

Palmer, Rupert E. Jr. "The Uses of Character in 'Bishop Blougram's Apology'." *Modern Philology,* 58 (1960): 108 – 18.

Priestley, R. E. L. "Blougram's Apologetics." *University of Toronto Quarterly*. 15 (1946): 139 – 47.

Raymond, William O. *The Infinite Moment and Other Essays in Robert Browning*. Toronto: Univ. of Toronto Press, 1950.

Rogers, Christopher Joseph. "Self-Reflexivity in Robert Browning's Poetry." An Unpublished Dissertation. The University of Toledo, 1983.

Shapiro, Arnold. "A New (Old) Reading of Bishop Blougram's Apology: The Problem of the Dramatic Monologue." *Victorian Poetry*, 10 (1972): 243 – 56.

Shaw, W. David. *he Dialectical Temper: The Rhetorical Art of Robert Browning*. Ithaca, New York: Cornell Univ. Press, 1968.

Slinn, E. Warwick. *Browning and the Fictions of Identity*. Totowa, NJ: Barnes & Noble Books, 1977.

Thomas, Donald. *Robert Browning: A Life Within Life*. New York: Viking Press, 1982.

19세기 영미시인들의 소통에 대한 욕구

인쇄일 초판1쇄 2008년 8월 25일
발행일 초판1쇄 2008년 8월 30일
지은이 조병은 / **발행인** 정구형 / **발행처** *L. I. E.*
등록일 2006. 11. 02 제17-353호

서울시 강동구 성내동 447-11 현영빌딩 2층
Tel : 442-4623,4,6 / Fax : 442-4625
homepage : www.kookhak.co.kr
e-mail : kookhak2001@hanmail.net
ISBN 978-89-93047-03-5 *94800 / 가 격 13,000원
978-89-959111-5-0 *94800 (set)

L. I. E. (Literature in English)